Brooklyn to Yellowstone
A 1933 Civilian Conservation Corps Odyssey

Michael LoMonico

Publisher: Vox Veritas

"Life is divided into three terms—that which was, which is, and which will be. Let us learn from the past to profit by the present, and from the present, to live better in the future." William Wordsworth

"After you have finished your true stories sometime, why don't you make up a story and the people that go with it? Only then will you understand what happened and why. It is those we live with and love and should know who elude us." Norman Maclean

"Get your facts first, and then you can distort 'em as much as you please." Mark Twain

"What's past is prologue." William Shakespeare

To my father, Michael C. LoMonico 1913-1965. Using the words in your journal as inspiration, I've taken great liberties and added my words to create the character you might have been.

Michael LoMonico 1933

And to my son, Michael, my daughter, Maura, and my grandchildren, Michael, Jake, and Ella. I lost my father when I was a mere lad of nineteen, so I hope his words and mine bring you to that certain time and place in history.

Contents

Prologue

B etween 1900 and 1914, almost two million able-bodied Italian men and women left Palermo, Messina, Naples, and other Southern Italian cities, searching for a better life. They settled in what became known as a "Little Italy" in many major cities in America, including Chicago, Boston, Philadelphia, New Jersey, Baltimore, and the five boroughs of New York City. These Italian immigrants tended to preserve the isolation they experienced in their villages in their new country by clustering together in close enclaves. In some cases, the population of a single Italian village ended up living on the same block.

In my parents' case, it was the Lower East Side of Manhattan where about one million of Italy's diaspora set root. My own and other families were helped by *Ordine Figli d'Italia* or the Order of the Sons of Italy, an organization which supported Italian immigrants who needed housing or financial aid and helped them assimilate into America. With their help, my parents soon secured affordable housing in an area called East New York in Brooklyn, where I was born in August of 1913.

Like most immigrants, Italians were able to bring very few material goods from their hometowns. Nevertheless, they still had a profound impact on New York City's cultural landscape. Their culinary traditions enriched the city's gourmands, bringing pizza and pasta to America. Their love for traditional folk music, like tarantella and opera, enriched the local music scene. They celebrated saints' days with elaborate *"festas"* or religious feasts, further sharing Italian food, music, pageantry, and games.

I grew up knowing that Sicilian culture's emphasis on family ties meant respect for my elders. Families were close-knit units essential for support and security in this challenging new world. Parents shaped their children, especially their sons, through unwritten rules. These rules were those our elders were raised with. They were designed to help young Italian men navigate the challenges of life in a new country.

I call them *Brooklyn Rules*.

Brooklyn Rules were based on a few core principles: young Italian men had to be respectful and obedient to their parents. They had to be hard-working and responsible, and were expected to defend their families against any threats.

Brooklyn Rules were not always easy to follow. These young men faced many challenges, and in the 1930s when I was coming of age, that included poverty, discrimination, and crime. Non-Italians had lots of derogatory words to describe us, and they weren't afraid to use them in public. Even in school, many teachers favored those kids whose names were easier to pronounce and who spoke better English than we did. However, our *Brooklyn Rules* provided us with a set of unique values that helped us to overcome these challenges and give us comfort. We knew what was expected of us. And we did it... or we were out in the cold.

As a 19-year-old, the *Brooklyn Rules* that I followed without question were:

•A young man should never leave Brooklyn even though his parents left our hallowed homeland.

•He must go to school in Brooklyn, preferably at a parish Catholic school, up to 8th grade unless his family is wealthy, in which case, he shall attend a private or public high school.

•He must get a job in Brooklyn to help support his family, especially due to the Great Depression.

•He must date only Italian girls, preferably from the neighborhood.

•He must not have sex with any of these girls, since he might end up marrying one of them.

•Upon selection of the requisite Italian wife, he must marry in Brooklyn.

•He and his wife must rent an apartment in Brooklyn until they can afford a house close to the groom's parents' home, and have children.

•Divorce is not an option.

I should point out that these were **my** Brooklyn rules, but I'm sure there were Brooklyn rules for Polish immigrants in Greenpoint, Eastern European Jews in Brownsville, German immigrants in Williamsburg, and similar rules for Italians all across America.

The Civilian Conservation Corps would pay me a dollar a day, most of which would automatically be sent to my family. There were no jobs at home that would pay anything close to that. What follows is my attempt to adhere to these rules, while navigating life outside of my hometown thanks to the CCCs in the summer of 1933.

B ut in my very next chapter, I break an important rule about the family's privacy.

Part One
Brooklyn

Rule 1
Keep Family Matters Private

Tuesday, June 6, 1933: Into Montana and Yellowstone

The train was going along pretty fast for a few hours till we came to a Wonderful town called Livingston which I'll never forget as long as I live. The train stopped for the night. They gave some of us leave until 5 A.M. and then the fun began. We first visited a saloon just like one in the movies, a long bar, a rickety piano playing, some old guys playing cards, and for the first time I started to realize I was really in the West. I gave the man behind the bar a $5 bill and he gave me change in Silver Dollars.

Then we went to a section of town called B Street and there I saw things I never saw before, which I can't explain in this book. Then we went to a cafeteria for a bite to eat, where I met the sweetest girl in the West. Her name was Marie Grasse. She was very nice and pleasant to talk to. She got stuck on my style, so I walked out with her and learned she was stopping at the Northern Hotel in Livingston. I went up to her suite (2 rooms) and had a very nice time, almost missed my train which left at 5:15.

Sunday, August 8, 1965

To my sons, Michael, Charles, and Larry,

This passage is from the private journal I kept over 30 years ago about my time in the CCCs in Yellowstone National Park. I remember buying that notebook for five cents on the day I enrolled. At the time, I thought it would be a way to document what this adventure would be like. Of course, the guys used to tease me about my obsession with writing, and some of them started refer-ring to me as Shakespeare. I never intended to share my comments, but since all this time has passed, now is the time. Reading this sample entry from 1933, you might have some questions:

- What did I actually witness in Livingston, Montana?
- What did I experience on B Street that night?
- What happened between me and Maria Grasse?
- And what were the rest of those months in Yellowstone like?

This is a story I should have told you long ago, but your Mom would not have appreciated learning what I did that summer. Now that she has passed, I can break the first *Brooklyn Rule* and tell all. I wrote those words and many more in my journal, but I never shared them with you boys until now. I apologize for that. Yellow-stone changed my life and made me the man I became. Now that you three are adults, I can tell my story.

I'll start with the stock market that crashed in October 1929, causing the Great Depression. Its effects lingered for what seemed like forever—about a quarter of the country's workforce lost their jobs. The suicide rate was at an all-time high. More than two million men and women lost their houses and took to the rails. Many were teens like me who left their homes in search of work.

Many traveled illegally and dangerously in or on top of the boxcars of freight trains. The press started calling them "hobos," a name that either derived from "homeless boys" or "homeward bound," depending on which version you heard. And they soon became universally known as "The Boxcar Kids." When their plan of finding jobs didn't happen, they set up makeshift camps called "Hoovervilles," named after Herbert Hoover, the president who most people felt led us into this mess. I didn't want to end up like them.

I n the winter of 1933, the dark cloud of the Great Depression continued to hang heavy over Brooklyn. I saw empty boarded-up storefronts with faded "for rent" signs hanging in their windows; long bread lines of people, bundled in worn clothing, waiting for a meager meal, and other desperate folks lined up at the soup kitchen at St. Fortunata's church.

I stood 5'7" and weighed a mere 130 pounds, I was lost and adrift. I had a crappy job selling newspapers, but I didn't earn enough money to help the family. When my father lost his tailoring job at Bloomingdales, our life changed. We eventually started to get welfare checks from the government, which humiliated us. That and our little backyard vegetable garden got us through each day. We wore hand-me-downs. We had our radio, though my father often talked about pawning it. We convinced him not to, as it was our only means of entertainment. Since I was the oldest in the family, the pressure was on me to earn a decent salary. I kept trying but couldn't get a real job. I had no idea about my future. Sure, I had dreams and ambitions like any young person, but the reality of the world around me felt overwhelming and insurmountable. The future was grim; there was no end in sight to the suffering.

But then, I joined the Civilian Conservation Corps, and everything changed. The CCCs weren't what I expected.

Suddenly, I had calluses on my hands from gripping a shovel all day, and muscles I never knew existed ached after a day of hauling logs. But the real change was deeper.

There I was, someone who wouldn't have dared climb a tree before, now scaling a giant oak. Other times, beads of sweat dripped from my brow as I swung an axe at stubborn undergrowth. Some days, the smell of smoke choked the air, signaling a raging wildfire, devouring everything in its path. I joined an army of shovels and hoses, battling the inferno. I didn't have time to be afraid.

The CCC wasn't just a job; it was a crucible. It forged me into a man, not just with stronger muscles, but with a stronger spirit. I learned the value of hard work, the thrill of facing my fears, and the bond forged in working with other men. It was under that Big Sky in Montana, surrounded by all that nature, that I truly found myself.

I became a man, both physically and emotionally.

As I think back, that experiences led to my current job of Coca-Cola District Sales Manager for all of Suffolk County. Yellowstone was where I became a leader of men, rather than a follower of boys, which I had been back in Brooklyn. On the train ride from New York to Montana, I was selected to be in charge of the Pullman car and depending on the train, I often got to stay in a private compartment. While I had been angry at the government for allowing the Depression to happen, I was thankful every day for what FDR created, giving me a chance to become a CCC man. My relationship with authority changed from one of derision to one of respect. The day I arrived in Yellowstone, I was appointed foreman of our camp.

Out West, things changed. Boyish crushes faded. Maybe it was the hard work or the wide-open spaces, but I craved something more lasting. Back home, there was always pressure to settle down. Under the stars, that didn't seem so bad anymore. It was time to stop chasing and find something real. As you will see, I had many girlfriends back home and met even more women out

West, but I eventually realized that I needed to settle down and take on the life I was expected to live. It's the Brooklyn Rule. And that's what I did.

Last month, while cleaning out the attic, I found the dusty, hand-made wooden trunk I had when I joined the CCCs. I had put it in the attic in 1950, when we left Brooklyn and bought our house in suburbia. After getting married, becoming a father 3 times, and all kinds of job-related issues, I had mostly forgotten about it and had long ago lost the padlock key. It took me a while to hacksaw it off.

Inside was my souvenir haul from Yellowstone. First, there was a varnished elk antler, a reminder of all the majestic elk I'd seen roaming the park. I bought it at the general store, a place that probably saw countless visitors like me snatching up mementos. Right next to the antler, was a rolled-up blue and gold CCC banner. I'd purchased it from the same store just before leaving camp, a tribute to the experience I'd had with the program. The trunk also contained some of the day-to-day items I used that summer: a World War I surplus army mess kit and canteen for when we were away from camp fighting forest fires, a toothbrush, a comb, a pair of leather boots, a dress uniform, some wrinkled shirts and work pants, a series of documents acknowledging my CCC service, a stack of old letters wrapped in string, and that five-cent notebook I kept during the Spring and Summer of '33.

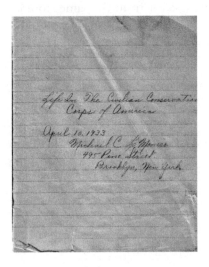

I stopped what I was doing, sat right down on the old trunk, and read that journal from beginning to end. It has been over 30 years, and reading my words brought me back to part of my youth that was truly the best of times and the worst of times.

Charles Dickens was referring to the French Revolution when he used that expression, but for me, a young kid, coming of age in the middle of the Great Depression, it feels like an appropriate way to describe my life in the Civilian Conservation Corps in 1933.

Reading my own words across the years and hearing my 19-year-old voice was surprising and enlightening. Some passages gave me the chills; others made me sad. Now I could relive it with my own actual words describing those events. It was almost surreal.

All these years later, so many specific moments and images resurfaced. I can recall the camp where we lived, the crisp Yellowstone air I breathed in almost every morning, the sounds of the trees being cut down, and, unfortunately, the stench of the forest fires we fought. But most of all, I felt free and alive in a way I hadn't been for a long time, and, to tell the truth, free and alive like I have not been since. I'm not saying I made the wrong decision. Obviously, you three would not exist if I didn't come home. But you get the idea.

I think back to my friends from that adventure, both tried-and-true ones from the old neighborhood like Jimmy and Mario, and the girls back home, Pauline and Terry. I remember my newfound friends from places like Wyoming, California, Idaho, and Hawaii. And of course, I remember our leaders, one, an ex-military sergeant who was both nasty and deranged, and those officers and other NCOs who were smart and supportive. And finally, there were those I loved and those I lost during our six-month adventure.

But the most vivid memory is of the one I left behind.

I am writing this book to show what I omitted—details I thought probably shouldn't be written in a journal. This is the story the nineteen-year-old me wouldn't write, but the one that deserves to be told. It's all true, every messy detail, every wild experience. This is my unvarnished past, laid bare. And it will all be true.

The major event I tried to forget about those six months was the death of a dear friend. I had never seen a dead body before, and it was a picture I couldn't get out of my mind. I felt repulsion, anger, and especially sorrow.

Some of my experiences I never shared with your mom either. But it's time for me to write how I became a man, so you three boys can know my odyssey and share it with your kids.

As best I could, I will try to replicate some of the events and take liberties with some of the dialogue. The book will give you, as well as other readers, insight into the Great Depression and the CCCs.

But first, I contacted the few local surviving CCC mates I could find to pick their brains on what they could recall. I hadn't stayed in touch with any of them, and it wasn't so easy to track them down. Once I found the directory of our unit, the telephone book was a big help. Reuniting with Sal Romano, Roberto Monteleone, and Anthony Setteducati, who all live nearby has been such a thrill. We still meet every Sunday morning at Strathmore Bagels to reminisce and tell old tales. They were essential in filling in the gaps about the wonderful and tragic events I had tried to forget.

But my story begins in Brooklyn when I was in 8th Grade.

I think I first became a writer when I was in 8th grade in PS 253, thanks to Miss Reed. The composition topic she assigned was "What do you want to do when you grow up?" I wrote my essay on how I would love to travel the world, starting with my parents' hometown in Sicily. Then I added I would love to live in Rome and Paris. I would love to travel to Cuba and Alaska and Hollywood and the Grand Canyon, and whatever else I could think of to fill up the required 250 words. I thought about going to all those places someday, and I even added a sentence for each place about why I wanted to go there. My favorite sentence was the one about Sicilian villages. "I think when I get to Sicily, I will meet a beautiful bride who is a wonderful cook and bring her home to Brooklyn." I remember Miss Reed wrote "*Wanderlust*" on my paper.

"Excuse me, Miss," I said to her as I pointed to her writing. "What does *wanderlust* mean?

"Well, Michael, you certainly have it," she said. "Look it up tonight."

"Yes, Ma'am. Thank you."

She gave me a big smile and inscribed my paper with an A, along with the words, "Michael, you are a brilliant writer, filled with *wanderlust*." She was tall, young, and so pretty, especially compared to the nuns I had had before I changed schools in the seventh grade. And I learned so much in her class, especially with the books she had us read. One of my favorites was *Last of the Mohicans,* which took place in Upstate New York and told the story of Hawkeye and his friend, the Mohawk Indian chief, Chingachgook. It was a swell book with lots of action and adventures. I also liked *The Call of the Wild* by Jack London, which was about a dog named Buck who is stolen from a ranch in California and sold as a sled dog in Alaska during the Gold Rush. I just loved reading about different places.

When I got home later, I looked up *wanderlust* in our old, yellowed *Webster's Dictionary*. It was between "wandering Jew" (which is actually a plant with striped leaves?) and "wanderoo" (a purple-faced monkey!) The definition of *wanderlust* read, "a strong longing for, yearning, or impulse toward traveling." Well, I guess that was me, all right. Whenever I read a book set in some far-off land, it was on my mind for days. When I read Zane Grey's *Riders of the Purple Sage,* I felt like I was in the dusty streets of the Wild West, or I felt like I was on the Mississippi while reading Mark Twain's *Adventures of Huckleberry Finn.* I am also a big fan of the movies, and whenever I saw one in some exotic locale, I would dream about going there someday.

When I was young, I'd go to the library several times a month to read books about cities like Paris, London, Lisbon, and Madrid, as well as books about New Orleans, San Francisco, Boston, and a few others. The ones I picked included lots of photographs and many even included maps. In my dreams, I made some serious plans to become a famous novelist and take on the world, but in 1929, eight years after I finished school in 8th grade, reality set in. I'd look around me and my family struggling through the damned Depression, and I knew I was destined to never leave Brooklyn and follow that first Brooklyn Rule.

Nobody ever leaves Brooklyn.

That was the one every Italian guy I knew lived by. The rest of it was pretty straightforward: you were born in Brooklyn of Italian immigrants; you went to school in Brooklyn, at least up to 8th grade; then you got a job in Brooklyn; next you met your Italian wife and got married in Brooklyn, and after living in your parents' house, you rented an apartment in Brooklyn, and then had children and bought a house preferably next door to your parents in Brooklyn. Was it possible for me to dare break it?

When I was 18, I figured it out. I had seen it happen to my uncle Ralph, Jimmy's brother, Franco, and my next-door neighbor, Carlo. I guess they all seemed pretty okay. But I wasn't sure it was my path. There had to be more to my existence than living and dying in Brooklyn. I wanted to break the rule. I just didn't know how to do it.

Rule 2
Contribute to the Household

They used to tell me I was building a dream,
And so I followed the mob.
When there was earth to plow, or guns to bear,
I was always there, right on the job.

They used to tell me I was building a dream, with
*   peace and glory ahead.*
Why should I be standing in line, just waiting for
*   bread?*
Once I built a railroad, I made it run, made it race
*   against time.*
Once I built a railroad; now it's done. Brother, can
*   you spare a dime?*

Once I built a tower up to the sun, brick and rivet
*   and lime.*
Once I built a tower, now it's done. Brother, can you
*   spare a dime?*

Once in khaki suits, gee, we looked swell,
Full of that yankee doodle dum.

Half a million boots went sloggin' through Hell,
And I was the kid with the drum!

Say don't you remember?
They called me Al. It was Al all the time.
Why don't you remember?
I'm your pal. Say buddy, can you spare a dime?

—Songwriters: E. Y. Harburg / Jay Gorney

T he "Great Depression" had reached 495 Pine Street in 1930, when my father lost his job as a tailor at Bloomingdale's after being with them for 10 years. I knew the depression started with the banks and Wall Street and some other government institutions, and for the previous two years, everyone seemed to point their finger at someone else. Personally, the who or the how or the why meant nothing to me. What mattered was what me and my family had to live through each day to make ends meet. The only breaks we had were some government food help or "relief" as they called it, listening to the radio, and going to the movies.

My father came to America in 1910 from a little town in Sicily called San Cataldo. There must have been some miscommunication at the dock in Palermo or Ellis Island because even though his real name is Frank, his immigration papers list his name as Cataldo LoMonico. Since he spoke no English, he didn't know how to object, and Cataldo became his official name. Everyone called him Frank or Franco or sometimes, Mr. Frank. He was a tailor, and a damned good one. Until August 1930, he was happy fitting and altering men's suits, but as the Depression continued, rich folks weren't buying fancy $25 suits anymore. Those days, he spent most of his time alone in his own personal depression, simply staring out the window in his rocking chair from morning until night in the front room of our Brooklyn house.

My mother came to America in 1911, married my father, and spent all of her time taking care of us five kids. She had been a baker before she married, so we didn't have to stand in the bread lines too often.

In 1932, they diagnosed Larry with tuberculosis, so your grandma devoted a lot of time caring for him. At first, he had a cough that didn't seem to go away. He felt sick and weak and started to lose weight. Then Dr. Amato came to the house and told us that he had TB. Of course, we couldn't afford to send him to a sanatorium, so Larry spent much of his time in the backyard or in the back bedroom. Even so, he kept getting fevers and would awake many times with night sweats. Sometimes, he would be coughing up blood. It was so hard to see him in that condition.

Sammy was only twelve, and he had been getting into all kinds of minor trouble, so I was always worried about him. He and his friends, who we said were a bad influence on him, did stupid things like throwing rocks at passing buses or taking stuff from Izzy's candy store around the block.

Fanny sold apples at the bus station each day. She got the apples for two cents each from the farm in the Old Mill and sold them for a nickel. The people taking the subway had jobs, and so they were kind when they bought one from her. Some people felt sorry for her and just gave her the nickel.

Grace was the only one who had an actual job, working in the gift shop on the 84th floor of the amazing new Empire State Building. She had a boyfriend named Angelo who always seemed to have money. He helped Grace get a job in the city and she supported all of us.

And then there's me. When I was sixteen, I tried my hand at barber school with some money my folks had saved up, but soon after October 29, 1929, I couldn't find work at any shops. I even tried pawning my scissors, but Morris at the pawnshop offered me so little that I kept them. So, then I sold the *Brooklyn Daily Eagle* and *The New York Times* at the subway entrance across the street from where Fanny sold her apples.

My friend Jimmy Cala, who worked next to me, sold the *Daily News* and the *Herald Tribune*. Jimmy lived on Pitkin Avenue, a few blocks from my house, and we'd been friends since kindergarten. People said we were like brothers because we went everywhere together.

Working with Jimmy did make the time go by with his constant joking and the way he would speak to his customers. He would say, "Good morning young lady" to most women despite their ages. And he would try to entertain them by complimenting their apparel or mentioning an article in each day's paper that might appeal to women. He might say, "Tonight is the grand opening of Radio City Music Hall at Rockefeller Center," or "Inside today's *Herald Tribune,* there's an economic recipe for creamed fish with vegetables and stewed tomatoes." For the men, he would tip his cap, and say things like "You are looking dapper this morning, sir" or "I hope you have a successful day at the office." And to help sell papers, he would report the baseball scores as well as boxing news. I really grew to like Jimmy.

We had to be at the stop at 5:30 each morning before the noisy old truck dropped off a load of papers. They sold for three cents each and I earned half a penny for each one I sold. On a good day, I could sell all 50 papers, and I could earn a quarter. How the hell was I going to get anywhere at that rate?

Rule 3
Respect Your Country's Leaders

The Depression invented Wednesday Dish Night. Our theater was the Brooklyn Rialto, where for the price of admission (five cents), we'd see a newsreel, a short subject, maybe a cartoon, and whatever feature film was playing. Everyone left with a piece of white bone China—a salad dish, a soup plate, or perhaps a sugar bowl. Well, not everyone got free dinnerware. You had to be female.

My girlfriend Pauline was intent on getting a complete service for her family of six, so it became a weekly ritual for us and a regular cheap date.

"I hope you're planning on going to the movies with me on Wednesday, Duke," Pauline would ask. She called me Duke when she wanted something, and this time, it was all about the dishes.

"Oh, sure," I'd say. "I know your parents are counting on you."

We had gone for a walk and then we were having a soda at the candy store on Saturday afternoon. "Well, maybe when we get them a full set, we can start a collection for our house."

I hated when she said stuff like that because I wasn't ready to think about marriage. All I could say was, "OK."

There was a Wednesday Dish Night ritual each week. When

the movie was over, the crowd headed for the exit. There the ushers would stand on chairs or ladders, unloading wooden boxes, tossing straw and crushed up newspapers all over the lobby, and giving each woman what she came for. On April 2nd, Pauline scored a cup and saucer.

But one Dish Night began a momentous series of events. The movie was *If I Had a Million,* and I'll tell you about it in a bit. The show began with a funny cartoon based on the "Popeye, the Sailor" comic strip. I had been reading those comics for years, so seeing him on the screen, eating his spinach, fighting with Bluto, and speaking love with Olive Oyl was a treat.

Then came the newsreel, which was all about President Roosevelt's inauguration. It started with how this movie got to us so quickly, which was quite a feat. As soon as the ceremony, the speech, and the parade were over, they developed the film, put it on reels, rushed the reels onto a plane, and flew the reels to New York where trucks drove copies to our theater and others in the area. The newsreel showed cars and planes and aerial shots of NYC, and trucks rushing to make it happen. Since television had not been invented yet, it was pretty neat seeing an event that just happened a few days earlier, unlike today where we can watch the whole event live on television.

I liked what the President said in his speech. There he was in his top hat and striped pants and fur-lined jacket. We saw clips of him in a parade both before and after the ceremony in an open-topped car alongside President Hoover. The top hat was a sort of prop, as he kept waving it at the crowd gathered along the street.

But his *Inaugural Address* got to me.

I'll never forget Roosevelt saying, "Let me assert my firm belief that the only thing we have to fear is... fear itself—nameless, unreasoning, unjustified terror which paralyzes needed efforts to convert retreat into advance." How appropriate. Everyone I knew was living in fear.

He compared the Great Depression to an invasion by the enemy and used the language of wartime to explain the powers he planned to use to protect the USA. When the newsreel was over, the audience actually applauded, something which never happened before in my years of movie-going. Compared to Calvin Coolidge and Herbert Hoover, FDR had a plan and sounded decisive. I was only 19, so I hadn't been old enough to vote, but I felt so confident he would get us out of this mess. Listening to him made me hopeful. I hadn't felt hopeful in a long time. I squeezed Pauline's hand and pulled her close to me.

Then came the main feature, *If I Had a Million*, starring Gary Cooper, George Raft, W.C. Fields, and lots of other excellent actors. The main guy was a dying old billionaire. He was angry and tired of his greedy, money-hungry relatives, so he gave million-dollar checks to random strangers picked out of the phone book. The first name selected was John D. Rockefeller— Really. We all laughed. So, he tried again and picked nine different people. In the letter he sent with the check, he told them there were no conditions or restrictions attached to its use. But he cautioned them to use the money wisely for their own happiness and welfare. But it's a comedy, so you can probably guess what happened. Pauline and I laughed a lot and had a good time.

One episode was called "The Clerk" with Charles Laughton. While at a boring desk job in a giant room with lots of other guys doing similar tedious jobs, he receives his check and shows no emotion. He simply leaves his desk, calmly climbs the stairs to the office of the secretary of the president, then to the office of his private secretary, and finally knocks on the door of the president himself. When he admits himself, he blows a raspberry at his boss and quits. The audience cheered for that one.

We liked the episode called "Road Hogs" with W.C. Fields and some actress we didn't know who played Emily. Emily works in a restaurant and, after saving her money, buys a shiny brand-new Ford Coupe. She and Fields take it out for a drive, but almost immediately someone goes through a stop sign and wrecks it. When she gets her mysterious million-dollar check, she and Fields go out and buy eight clunky used cars. They hire some drivers and on one day, as soon as they see a terrible driver, they crash into that car. When they run out of cars, with the money left, Emily purchases a fancy new car. But guess what? It gets into a collision with a truck and is totally destroyed. Even though she is broke, Emily laughs and tells Fields she has had "a glorious day."

"I just love tonight's dish set," Pauline said, clutching her cup and saucer. "In a few more weeks I'll have completed two dinner place settings."

"Uh huh," was all I was able to say, because that whole movie stayed on my mind for days. As I said, before the stock market crash hit the economy, I had lots of grand dreams. I wanted to travel and see the world, own the shiniest Cadillac as soon as it came out, write lots of novels and go to Hollywood and make movies, and be rich and leaving Brooklyn behind. But now, I sold three-cent newspapers every morning and every night. And the prospect of getting out of here seemed impossible. But all Pauline could think about was those damned dishes, as if the movie went right over her head. And unlike what Emily said at the end of the movie, since this lousy Depression began, I had yet to have a "glorious day."

I looked back to last Sunday's *Brooklyn Eagle* which included the president's entire speech. I read it and found so much to give me hope. He said, "A host of unemployed citizens face the grim problem of existence and an equally great number toil with little return. Only a foolish optimist can deny the dark realities of the moment." Well, that was me and my family. Then he talked about the greedy leaders of Wall Street.

"They have no vision, and when there is no vision, the people perish." I couldn't follow all of what he said next, but near the end he said, "Restoration calls, however, not for changes in ethics alone. This Nation asks for action, and action now. Our greatest primary task is to put people to work."

Put the people to work all right. That's what we needed. So that's how our family would survive. It began to change on March 12, 1933.

Rule 4
Be Part of Something Larger

I t was bitterly cold on my way back from my paper station that evening. The sidewalk was coated with ice, making the trip from the subway stop to my home treacherous. The 10-minute walk had taken nearly twice as long, and the holes in my shoes had turned my socks into wet, cold sponges. I knew what awaited me at home—my poor father, still sitting in his chair by the front window, staring towards nowhere and my mother in the kitchen trying her best to keep us fed. Grace would already be home, Sammy off with his friends, and Larry, poor Larry, in the back bedroom. As I turned left onto Pine Street from Sutter Avenue, I saw my father, just like he had been every day for the past six months.

"It's freezing out for the middle of March," I said. "How are you doing, Pop?"

"*Menza menz*," he said, which was an improvement on his usual condition.

"There's a big talk on the radio tonight. The President is speaking to the entire country." He looked away, saying nothing.

Before the crash, my father surprised us one night with that beautiful Philco Cathedral-style radio. There were some questions about whether or not it had "fallen off a truck," a local expression for a stolen appliance, purchased from some random guy on the street. But my dad claimed he paid full price for it. Once the depression hit, it remained one of the few family luxuries we had. I think it was called "cathedral" because of its church-like shape, but we felt when we sat down to listen to one of our favorite shows, it was like attending Sunday Mass. I think part of the reason he bought it was so he and my mother could learn English. My friend Santo's family had one of those giant radios that sat on the floor, but ours was half that size and sat on a table next to the living room sofa.

Our favorite family shows were *The Ed Sullivan Show, The Carnation Contented Hour, The Jack Benny Program*, and George Burns and Gracie Allen on *The Guy Lombardo Show*. Those family shows consisted mostly of music and some comedy skits. It was OK, but we kids loved to listen to *Tarzan of the Apes. Buck Rogers in the 25th Century*, and *Charlie Chan*. These were 15-minute serials, and we couldn't get enough of them.

On that chilly March night, the new president was doing something he called a "fireside chat" on the radio. Of course, we didn't have a fireplace, but at precisely 8:00 p.m. I had all of us gather by the Philco to hear what FDR had to say. He talked a lot about banks and the stock market, which must have been important, but which meant little to me or the rest of the family. But then he mentioned the formation of what he called the "Civilian Conservation Corps" or the CCCs. It would be a program for young, unskilled unemployed men between the ages of 18 and 25 whose families were on relief. My ears perked up.

"That's me," I said to everyone in the room. They all laughed.

"No, really. I'm not kidding. This could be my ticket out of here, earning some actual money."

"You're right," said Grace. I knew she would be happy for me. "You should go sign up right away!" Your grandma gave her a dirty look.

"*Aspetto un momento*," she said. "That's something we all need to talk about."

"But mama," said Grace. "This would be good for Michael."
Mama just scowled.

"I know, but it sounds like a great idea," I said. "I'll probably get all the details in tomorrow's paper, and see if it makes sense."

"You may be 19, but you still live in this house, *filio mia*. Your father and I will decide what's good for you."

Next morning, when the truck dropped off the papers, Jimmy Cala and I scanned the front-page article, and learned we would be paid $1.00 a day or $30 a month, but $20-$25 would be sent directly to our families. We both qualified since both of our families were on government assistance or what they called "Relief." Most of the locations were in national parks across the country. And we would be in the CCCs for six months. If we passed the physical, we'd be in!

"Hey, Duke. Are you sure your mother and father are alright with this?" Jimmy asked. "From what I've seen, your mother is one tough lady."

"I know. Family is so important to her, and she would never let me just leave on my own. But when she sees how much money the family will get each month, she may change her mind. And I know Grace will help me convince her. How about your parents?"

"To be honest, I think they'd be happy to get rid of me."

"Really? Why do you think so?"

"They keep trying to fix me up with some girls with the idea that I would marry them and get out of their hair. "Tessie Maggio has a lovely daughter, Jimmy," my mother says. "Why don't you meet her?" Or "Mary Romanelli has a beautiful niece who just came over from Sicily. She's only 15, but you should ask her out?" They even say if I get married, it would be one less month to feed. That's what life is like in my house, Duke."

"Too bad we both don't have parents who are somewhere between mine and yours."

That night, I went to sleep feeling optimistic and alive for the first time in a long while. I didn't wait for my parents' approval. I knew I was being rebellious, but I wasn't a child now, and once I joined, they would realize it was a good thing. As soon as we sold our last morning papers the next day, me and Jimmy took the subway to Borough Hall to sign up.

When we got to the building, we saw a long line out the front door. We met some guys we knew, and everyone seemed to be in a good mood. One guy I saw was Salvatore Macchia's little brother, Tony. I knew he was only 16, but he was here anyway. I learned later that lots of kids used fake IDs to join, and Tony did get accepted.

After about an hour, we got to the head of the line and met with a pretty woman in her early 20s at a table. She asked us a bunch of questions—our names, addresses, parents' names, and names of brothers and sisters. Then she told us all we had to do was report to Whitehall Street for a physical the following week, and if we passed, we'd be notified when we should report to the Army Base at the Brooklyn Navy Yard. It all seemed so easy, but if my mother agreed, this could be the thing that would change my life. I decided to not say anything at home until I was actually accepted. Then I would deal with my mother.

As we started to leave, Jimmy kept smiling at her and said, "Now that you know my name, can you tell me yours, honey?"

She blushed and said, "Next."

But Jimmy wasn't leaving right away. "The government is going to send me far away for six whole months," he said, "And I will write to you every day if we can just go out one time. Won't you just tell me your name and phone number, sweetie?

At this point, I grabbed his arm and pulled him away. "Don't be such an asshole, Cala. She's not interested in what you've got to sell."

"Hey, Duke. You can't blame me for trying. You never know."

I should point out that as much as I liked Jimmy, he could be a pain in the ass. He was always coming on to any woman he met, and I was totally embarrassed. This had been his style since we were in 7th grade. My style was a lot different. I'd sort of stay back and let the girls come to me. In the end, I usually did better than him with the ladies. But that's another story.

Monday April 10, 1933
It took a few weeks, but we finally got the word to report to the base. After being re-examined at the Army Bldg. in N.Y.C., I was sent to the Army Base in Brooklyn. We were assigned to our bunks, then we had lunch. After lunch, we had stripped for another examination which was worse than the first. I couldn't sleep on account of the noise in the dormitory. Every time a sergeant came along someone razzed him. and my arm pained me from the injections they gave me in the afternoon. I fell asleep at 1:00 that night.

Tuesday April 11, 1933
Got up at 5:30 a.m. and it was pretty tough because I wasn't used to getting up so early, had breakfast which wasn't so hot, then went to the gymnasium had a little workout, came down wrote a few letters to some friends, played cards, lay around for the rest of the day. That night we all got passes to go home. Later, went to the club, came home about 12:00, went to bed.

On Monday, April 10, Jimmy and I headed to this gigantic Army building at 39 Whitehall Street in lower Manhattan, the place that all men entering the service reported to for their induction into the military. All I could think of was the thousands of GIs who walked through those halls before being shipped off to the Great War and how many of them never returned. It was chilling to think about the sacrifices they gave for their country. What we were doing was nothing in comparison.

After waiting a long time, they gave us a full physical examination to see if we were able to join the CCCs. And, yes, it was a full physical where they looked into every part of our bodies. Of course, Jimmy and I passed, and they sent us back to Brooklyn to an Army Base on the western shore of the East River.

We were officially members of the Civilian Conservation Corps.

I was amazed at the size of this base. When it was opened in 1924, the *Brooklyn Daily Eagle* called the base the "World's Largest Building." We were told to report to Warehouse A, an eight-story building which included administration offices, actual railroad tracks and actual railroad cars, two gymnasiums, a mess hall, as well as our barracks. The barracks was comprised of hundreds of cots, stretching as far as one could see.

They assigned Jimmy and me bunks, in row 23, next to each other. By then, we were starving and happy when they told us we were having lunch. The lunchroom was enormous, filled with hundreds of guys like us.

"Come sit here," some guy who was alone said, and we did. He said his name was Vincent and Jimmy and I told him our names. Vincent was a big guy with really curly hair. "The food's not too bad," he said, "but the coffee's lousy."

"I am starving," said Jimmy, "so I'll eat anything."

Vincent was already eating a ham and cheese sandwich on white bread. And pretty soon someone came by and gave us the same.

"I live in Flatbush," Vincent said. "Where are you guys from?"

"We're from East New York," I said, and Vincent laughed and reminded us how far away we would have to travel from each day that they let us go home. It would take us nearly two hours to get to the base, a route that would include walking, getting on the Fulton Street train, and taking a bus to the base on Second Avenue between 59th and 65th Streets. On most nights, we stayed on the base, but we often got home on weekends.

As we were getting ready to leave, I couldn't believe what

happened next. A server named Josh came to our table with a pile of sandwiches.

"You guys want some more?" he asked.

"Yes, we do," said Jimmy. We each took another. And then to make a joke, Jimmy asked, "By the way, Josh, what's for dessert?"

"I'll be right back," said Josh, and soon returned with several hefty slices of apple pie and more coffee.

"Do we get fed like this all the time?" I asked.

"You sure do. Wait until you see what's for dinner!"

Despite what Vincent had said, the coffee wasn't bad. The pie was delicious. I hadn't eaten that much in a long time. As I looked around, I noticed a lot of the guys near us looked pale and undernourished, and they were going for thirds. So many of the really poor families on Relief were starving. The bread lines helped and the Relief checks made a dent, but Nellie, my neighbor, would send her daughter to the butcher shop and ask for a bone for their dog (which they didn't have), and then Nellie would make soup from it. And a friend's father, to keep the apartment warm, often walked the railroad tracks to pick up coal fallen off trains coming into New York. So, sitting in that mess hall and seeing all that free food, made me think about the hungry folks all over the area.

After lunch, we had to strip for another examination, which, like I mentioned, was worse than the first. They probed everywhere and gave me several injections. They didn't even tell me what they were for, but they sure hurt.

Then around 4:00, we had to go to an assembly or, as they called it, *formation*. There were a bunch of welcoming remarks, and they thanked us for joining the Corps.

"You are now beginning, what we call boot camp," this tall officer said. He had a deep voice, and we all listened. "Although everything you will be going through might feel like you're in the army, you are still civilians, and can leave whenever you want." A lot of guys cheered, but no one seemed to go. "There is no penalty for leaving, though, of course, your family will no longer receive your monthly earnings." That brought a hush. "Here you will learn to live harmoniously in groups. You will be working very hard each day, completing dangerous tasks, and be relying on each other for survival."

Survival? That word struck me. I thought we would be doing light work in the parks, clearing brush, making paths, and planting trees. None of that seemed life-threatening. I started to wonder exactly what I had signed up for. The tall officer kept droning on, but I couldn't help wondering what I was in for. I glanced and Jimmy, but he didn't seem to be bothered by any of it. I guess he had the right idea. Of course, later on, we found out exactly how dangerous our service would be.

When our first dinner was served, I was speechless. Josh was right. The meal consisted of a huge, juicy steak, mashed potatoes, and string beans, along with some warm, fresh rolls. I had not had a steak in so long. I looked at it for a full minute before digging in. It was so delicious. I ate every bit, but I had to say no when Josh came by and offered me a second steak.

The day was long and hard, but I was excited. As Jimmy and I headed home that night, we agreed that signing up was the right decision. I knew enough to convince my mother that it was the right thing to do.

Rule 5
Be Reliable and Punctual

Wednesday, April 12, 1933

Got up at five o'clock for the second time that week, went back to Army Base at 7:00, cleaned up a little, listened to some boys play guitars and a mandolin. Passed a quiet day, went home again that night. Went down to the club, danced with some Girls, went home at 11:30 and went right to bed.

Thursday, April 13, 1933

Got up went to the Base that morning. I was assigned to K.P. at 10:00 for the first time, and it was awful. That day, we got our uniforms and undergarments. Later on, we were all brought down to the courtyard, and we all were sworn in. I met my ex-sweetheart on the train that night and talked to her for an hour. She told me I was crazy to join up with the Corps. I went home and went to bed.

I f I had any doubts about my decision to join the CCCs, the swearing-in ceremony settled it. I looked around at the 200 or more of us in this open area with our right hands raised. It was called the oath of enrollment and included lots of legal stuff about not being able to make claims against the government. But speaking those final words, 'So help me God' gave me goose pimples.

On the subway, I was nodding off when I was poked by my ex-girlfriend, Amelia. She and I had gone steady a few years earlier, until she broke it off. She was the prettiest girl I knew, and I still had feelings for her. She was tall, had curly black hair and was dressed in a gray suit wearing a red hat with a feather on it. To say the least, she was classy, probably too classy for me.

"Nice uniform, army boy, "she said. "Is there a war on that I don't know about?"

"I'm not in the army and you know it. Why do you have to make fun of me?"

"I'm not making fun. You do look handsome in that uniform."

"Thanks. I think that's a compliment."

"Just please tell me why you are doing this. If we're not fighting in a war, why work for the government? You should just get a nice job here."

"That's easy for you to say. You have a good job on Wall Street so you're lucky, but I gave up the daily grind of job searching. Selling newspapers isn't exactly a good career move for me."

That softened her up, and she tried to be nice to me. We continued to talk and after a while, she said that she would write to me. I thought she might be trying to tell me something like she wanted to get back together. As she was getting off at her stop, she gave me a quick kiss and said goodbye.

I was happy whenever they let us go home. I couldn't get to sleep at the base on account of the noise in the dormitory. Every time a sergeant came along, someone razzed him with muffled curses and nasty names.

The next day was pretty easy. We had a few more pep talks and lots of downtime. At 3:00, out of nowhere, they gave us passes to go home again. Jimmy and I left as quickly as we could, and we went straight to Jimmy's house.

Let me tell you more about Jimmy. He was handsome, stood about 5'6, with black hair and was stocky. Needless to say, the girls all loved him. His parents were friends with my family, and we sometimes had them over for cake and coffee on a Sunday afternoon, or they had us over. He was a year older than I was, and me and his sister Pauline had been seeing each other for a while. His older brother, John, had a 1928 Ford, so he would take us and a few boys all over. John asked us lots of questions about our decision to join the CCCs. I tried to convince him to join up because I was so sure that we had made the right decision. But did we?

Friday, April 14, 1933

Came in as usual, done my last morning K.P. Wrote some Postcards, had lunch. After that they took us to the courtyard and we got a good workout. Came up, played cards and got a special pass to go home that night. I met John Cala. We stayed down at the club, then about 10 o'clock John and some of the boys drove Jimmy and me to the Army Post and we had some sport coming down. The boys couldn't come up to the building, but we walked down to the dock and saw the S.S. Bremen, one of the prettiest boats on the Ocean. The boys went home, and I went to bed.

F irst of all, I hated KP, which was short for Kitchen Patrol and it meant "mess duty." Each of us got assigned to it several times. And if you did any kind of infraction, they used it as punishment. In addition to peeling potatoes, it could be dish washing and pot scrubbing, sweeping and mopping floors, wiping tables, or even serving food. When I left a session, my clothes stank and I was exhausted.

Seeing the *SS Bremen* was a surprise treat. It was a sleek, shiny German ocean liner, and as we stood on the pier, this enormous and beautiful ship stood out against the evening sky.

"The papers said that this ship was the largest, fastest, and most luxurious ship in the world," I said. "And I want to be on it, cruising across the Atlantic."

"Fat chance," said John Cala. "As far as I know, the CCCs aren't sending anyone on cruises to Germany or any place else in Europe. They might just be sending you guys to Upstate New York. Maybe just to Bear Mountain."

We had a good laugh at that, but I could always dream. Before signing up for the CCCs, I sometimes went to the public library and read magazines, especially "*Time*," but it mostly talked about the Depression and how it affected America as well as countries around the world. I had enough of that news.

But in one issue, there was a full-page ad for the Anchor Line, which had cruises from New York to Ireland and Scotland. That ad took me right back to my feeling of *wanderlust*, especially with phrases like, "luxury staterooms," "first class," and "undeniable distinction." These words were part of my dreams that might happen someday. So seeing the *Bremen* was especially emotional for me.

Saturday, April 15, 1933

*Got up as usual, had breakfast, after that we were made to line up
and they inspected our arms. Later, we had to clean up the place.
We later were given passes. At 12 o'clock we went home to come back
Monday. That day I went out, had a nice time, got to bed about 11
o'clock. Found that Vincent had left for Fort Hancock the day
before.*

We got to know some men who worked at the base. They
were not military, and they were a lot of fun to talk with.
One day we were sitting on boxes in a circle eating our sandwiches
with them and these old-timers told me and some of the guys a
little of this gigantic building's history. Although it was built to
hold supplies for the army during the war, it wasn't finished in
time. So now it held everything from surplus uniforms, ammuni-
tion, weapons, and machinery.

"Apparently," one of the old guys named Edgar told us, "the
army ran out of medicine and drugs to treat injured soldiers
during the war, so they built a vault to hold all the illicit narcotics
which would be used if there were ever another war. They told us
the army would not be caught short again."

"You mean they would use these drugs that they took from
gangsters for wounded soldiers," I asked.

"That's right. We get these drugs that are seized from various
courts around the country, and send them to the army medical
corps."

"What else is stored here?" I asked.

"One vault holds all the finest whiskey the government confis-
cated. Most of it came from the Customs Bureau. One time, they
seized 50,000 cases from a single ship. The rest came from the
New York Prohibition Force, which seized as much as $2,000,000
worth at a time."

"What are they going to do with all of it?" asked Jimmy.

"Well, initially, they installed an incinerator to destroy it all."

"Wait. They were burning the whiskey? Are you serious?" asked Jimmy.

"That was the plan," Arnie, another old-timer added. "But they soon realized that storing it was a better idea. "When the liquor arrives at the base, the bosses sample each shipment to see if it is any good. Tough job, right? If it was typical "rotgut," they emptied that shit into the East River."

"Are you kidding?" Jimmy said. "What nuts!"

"Well, they had so much of the good stuff they didn't think it was worth saving," said Arnie.

"Boy, I bet the fish all got drunk then," said Jimmy.

"Have you seen the East River?" asked Edgar. "No fish could have survived there before they dumped the alkie in. Anyway, the bosses took the good stuff and stored it in a safe in building A." He winked at Arnie.

"Sure, they did," said Arnie. "Bet they took a lot of it home for themselves first. But the real kicker was the gangsters who they took the booze from broke into the building and took it right back."

"That's right," added Edgar. "One group stole 122 cases of the finest Champagne; another stole 85 cases of 'medicinal' rye; and one, they called a daring inside job, removed 100 cases of whiskey seemingly without opening the vault."

"So, how did they stop them?

"They built these enormous vaults guaranteeing no more heists would happen."

We were still dealing with Prohibition while we were in training, but most New Yorkers knew how to get whatever they wanted. And we would soon find out Montana and Wyoming did not seem to know about the 19th Amendment, so we had as much booze as we wanted while we were away.

Rule 6
Embrace Your Family Traditions

Easter Sunday, April 16, 1933

Got up, dressed up, went to Church and met Pauline and Jimmy and a new kid named Mario. Went home, had a great dinner. The De Stephano's had dinner with us. After dinner, went out, talked to Chris D. for a few hours. Later went to Pete's house, stayed for an hour or so. Later went to the Club, then to the beer Garden and drank some beer. Then went riding with the boys. Went to bed about 1 o'clock. That was the end of a great day.

I t was a warm and sunny spring day, and I loved seeing so many young girls and older women wearing colorful Easter bonnets outside after church. I spotted Pauline in a yellow and pink straw hat with lots of ribbons on it. I walked over to her, and we talked for a while about my week and hers. Then, she gave me a quick peck on the cheek, and off she went.

Jimmy walked through the crowd with someone I didn't know and came over to me. "Hey, Mike, Happy Easter," he said.

"Our training has been mostly tedious and I can't wait until they tell us where the hell we're going."

"I agree, and Happy Easter to you and your family. Are you all eating at your house today?"

"Yeah. I want you to meet Mario, the guy I told you about. He had just moved into our neighborhood, but he joined the CCCs too. He's coming back to the base with us."

We shook hands and exchanged hellos. Mario was soft-spoken and seemed like a nice guy. He had reddish hair, freckles and spoke with the slightest stutter. I didn't realize it at the time, but he was to become one of my closest friends.

Being home for Easter was a treat. In preparation, mama had scrimped and saved and with Grace's help, and put on a feast for the ages. She had cleverly made a bartering deal with Nunzio, the neighborhood butcher. She agreed to bake about a dozen *torta pasqualina*, or what we now call Pizza Rustica, on Good Friday, in exchange for the meats she needed for our dinner. This Easter Pie was a deep-dish concoction packed with diced meats and cheeses like prosciutto, pepperoni, soppressata, mozzarella and provolone, along with a mixture of eggs and ricotta, all of which Nunzio would supply and sell on Holy Saturday. She even invited the De Stephano family, whose daughter was very sick and was having serious hardships. I was happy because their son, Chris, was a good friend.

The meal began with an antipasto, which included many of those same meats and cheeses along with olives, roasted peppers, anchovies, and artichoke hearts. Then came Mama's famous lasagna, followed by sausage, meatballs, and braciole, as well as a huge baked ham with all the trimmings. Dessert consisted of a huge tray of Italian pastry, including lots of cannoli. It felt like this was my last meal, and I knew no matter how good the food would be in camp, I would not see a meal like this for a very long time. After dinner, we sat in the living room and my father poured each of us a glass of his homemade Limoncello. Mama never said it, but I think she had finally come to terms with my decision, and Easter 1933 was my farewell dinner.

Later Chris suggested we go to Pete's house. "I don't know," I said. "My mom made this special dinner and I'd hate to aggravate her."

"We won't stay long, and she'll be busy listening to my mother's neighborhood gossip all afternoon."

"I know she'll be missing me when I go away for six months, but I guess it will be alright."

And so, we went and had a second dessert and stayed for an hour or so. Then the three of us went to the Club where we met Jimmy and a lot of the boys. The Club was our personal hangout when we wanted to get away from our folks. Actually, it was part of the taxi stand on Euclid Avenue where some of the old guys let us hang out. It was a place to meet, to have a smoke, and tell jokes.

That night, someone had the idea that we should all go to Trommer's Beer Garden and sing and drink some near-beer. A bunch of the girls joined us as well. It was amazing. People were on benches as far as we could see, the music was great, and although the beer was the weak 3.2 crap, we drank pitcher after pitcher of it. We sang old songs together and had a great time.

Later that night, I again started to second-guess myself and wondered if I had made the right decision. After all, I had such good friends and we had so many places to go and we had such a terrific group of girls. Why was I leaving all this?

Rule 7
Be Respectful of Women

Monday, April 17, 1933

Met the boys at Linwood St. Station at 5:30 a.m., came to Base at 6:45. Cleaned up and got lined up and got another injection in my right arm which was a honey. Got a letter from M.A. with sad news for me but it didn't bother me much. It was something that could be expected. Answered M.A. letter thanking her. Listened to lecture from Medical Surgeon about health and how to keep fit. Felt sick all afternoon on account of injections. Headed for home, and stopped to speak to Pauline, went home and got to bed at 9:15.

The beginning of the second week was difficult for me as I felt so sick. Perhaps it was all that eating and drinking over the Easter weekend, but it was a rough time. The doctor's lecture on Monday was supposed to be about nutrition, but he focused mostly about sex. Jim and Mario and I sat together for this.

"Good morning, boys," he began. "I'm here to talk to you about some important matters that concern your well-being. You should be proud of yourselves and your work in the CCCs. But you should also be careful and responsible. You see, there are dangers and temptations that lurk in the woods and in the towns that you will visit on your days off. And I'm not talking about bears or snakes or poison ivy. I'm talking about diseases that can ruin your health and your future."

He showed us some scary slides and talked for close to an hour discussing syphilis, gonorrhea, and hepatitis, trying to scare us all. "These diseases can cause pain, fever, sores, rashes, swelling, infertility, blindness, paralysis, insanity, and even death." So, he immediately had my attention, and my mind drifted off thinking about my girls.

I n my formative years (and even later) I must admit, I loved girls. I found them to be beautiful, charming, and interesting. I enjoyed spending time with them and getting to know them. I also enjoyed the physical side of relationships with girls, such as kissing and cuddling. I liked how they talked with me when we were alone, the way they smelled when I was near them, and the way their skin felt when I held them. Girls—all girls –were a big part of my everyday life growing up. I guess you could have called me a Ladies Man. And yet I was a virgin in the spring of 1933.

While the doc continued his lecture, I started reminiscing about some of the girls I had dated. I had thought about "going all the way" with any one of the girls before I left, but, for some reason that I do not remember, I had decided that I was "saving myself for marriage." I knew it was one of the unwritten and unspoken Brooklyn Rules. But, once I got away from Brooklyn, I was sure that would all change.

Here are some of the girls I dated before joining the Corps, most of whom would have had real sex with me if I wasn't such a jerk.

Terry was simply a blonde flirt who was completely obsessed with me. I went with her between Kate, and Pauline, but she was too clingy. We had a good time together, but after a few months, I had to break it off because she wanted to be with me constantly. She promised she'd write when I was away, probably because she had hopes of getting back together. I liked her letters and packages, but I knew that getting together wouldn't happen.

Louise used to hang out with me and the boys at the Club. She and I had a short fling because there was something about her voice and the way she spoke that got to me. She went to school at St. Fortunata's and sang in the choir. But the nuns messed up her mind about any kind of intimacy with a boy, so even heavy kissing was forbidden.

Amelia was the smartest neighborhood girl. She had graduated high school from Saint Saviour on 6th Street near Prospect Park. Her father was a lawyer, and she told me that she might go to law school someday. Since I had only finished 8th grade, I always felt dumb when we were together. But she was lots of fun to be with, and my lack of schooling never bothered her. She was working on Wall Street, so we gradually moved apart.

Pauline had been my most recent steady girlfriend. She was pretty and smart and kind of serious, and I liked spending time with her. She was upset when I told her that I would be gone for six months, and she kept pestering me about my decision. "Will you forget about me when you're gone?" was her constant annoying question. Later in May, she started meeting me at the station each morning, supposedly because she claimed she had a new job near Brooklyn Borough Hall. I was to find out later that she had no job, but only rode the train each morning so she could see me. That made me angry. But she was also the girl who went with me to Coney Island to see Baby Mary. I'll get to Baby Mary shortly.

Mary Ann was one of the sweetest girls I ever dated. She was petite and had a beautiful complexion. We got together when I was about 17, and we enjoyed being together. A few years after we stopped seeing each other, she dated Ronnie DeMarco. Then I heard that she had gone upstate to live with an aunt. In her letter I got that Monday, she told me that she had gotten pregnant and would have the baby where she was living with her aunt. We never saw her again. That made me wonder what Brooklyn Rules the girls had to follow.

This brings me back to the doctor's sex talk. As I look back on those days, I probably could have had a sexual relationship with most of them. Louise and her nuns might be an exception. And I had proof that Mary Ann would have been eligible.

When I got back to reality, the doc was finishing up. "Some of you may think that this doesn't concern you," he was saying. "That you are too young or too strong or too lucky to get VD. That you only have sex with clean girls or that you use protection or that you can tell if someone has VD by looking at them. Well, let me tell you something: none of that is true."

Jim rolled his eyes and said, "I have an excellent VD meter, so I can spot gonorrhea a mile away." Mario and I tried to hold our laughter at that. Jim was the only one of us who had sexual intercourse, and he had always encouraged us to do the same.

The lecture continued with mentions of leaky condoms, avoiding girls who look sick or dirty, and abstaining from sex until marriage. "You are part of a great generation," the doc said. "Don't let VD destroy your health and your dreams. Don't let VD be your enemy within."

The three of us didn't say much on the train ride home. I was still feeling pretty sick, so I closed my eyes and tried to get some sleep.

Tuesday April 18, 1933
Got up and felt very bad. Arrived at army base, felt worse. Took a physic then went to Doctor. He painted my throat with medicine. Felt better after dinner. An army transport arrived at the base with about 500 soldiers which made it uncomfortable for us for a while. Got a pass to go home. Met Jimmy De at the house. Went out. Spoke

to Louise P. Promised to write to her when I left. Went down to the club, fooled around until 11 o'clock. Went home and got to bed.

Wednesday April 19, 1933
Came in as usual, felt much better. Worked around a little, and was changed into another squad after a few arguments but finally consented. Soldiers were giving uniforms away. I got a shirt and 2 coats, 2 pair of breeches. Went home at 4:00, shaved, cleaned, went out to the club, met the boys and girls. Had some fun, and was taken back to army base by Jimmy Y. with the girls in the car. Arrived at Base at 12:30. Was very cold that night.

Thursday April 20, 1933
Got up with a cold, felt rotten all day long. Went to doctor, gave me some pills to take. Didn't do me any good. Worked around the place for a few hours then laid down while other boys went down to drill. I felt terrible. About 4 o'clock got a pass to go home. Went home, had supper. Willie Brown was over the house. We went to the show later and saw two good pictures. Got home at 11:30. My cold was worse. Took a rub down and went to bed.

Friday April 21, 1933
Was very sick in the morning. Did not get up to go to Army Base. Got up at 1:00, was out in the sun for the afternoon. Felt much better. Spoke to Pauline that night. Later went to the club, had some fun, went home about 10:00. Went to bed for the night.

That whole week is a blur for me now as I write this. I probably should tell you that I was pretty sick in those days leading up to leaving. I weighed only 140 lbs. I had gotten sick a lot when I was younger. I do think all the sickness I dealt with that week was due to the injections they kept giving us, though the other guys seemed to handle it better. You can also tell from what I wrote that feeling sick and my mother's pleading didn't always stop me from going out with my friends at night.

But after seeing me being so congested and miserable, your grandmother decided that she knew how to cure me. I left this out of my journal because I was a little embarrassed about her cure, which was based on an old wives' remedy, especially among Italian women, for whatever ailed a person. Here's how it went on that Friday night.

It was called "cupping." You see, cupping was a common treatment for a variety of illnesses, including colds, flu, pneumonia, and headaches. Old Italian mothers would often use cupping to treat their sick children.

To perform cupping, I had to get in my bed and lie on my stomach, while your grandma heated a glass cup over a candle flame. Once the cup was hot, she placed it on my back. It was really hot and stuck there using suction. She repeated this with about six or seven more cups and left me there for about 15 minutes. Supposedly, the suction created by the hot air would draw my blood to the surface of my skin, and get the bad stuff out. What it did was create a red mark and a series of huge bumps. The theory behind cupping is that the suction helps to draw out toxins and improve circulation.

Years later a friend told me that her Southern mother believed that the secret to getting rid of warts was to wrap a box full of rocks, tie a ribbon on it, and set it on the side of the road for a stranger to pick up. Then the warts would be transported to that person. Another old wives' tale I heard was that after a sick child falls asleep, the mother should cut an onion in half and put it next to the child's bed. One of the onion's qualities is that it absorbs bacteria and that child is magically cured.

I don't know how cupping worked, but the truth was that I felt better the next day, so maybe it worked.

Rule 8
Help Your Younger Siblings

Saturday, April 22, 1933

Got up as usual, felt much better than the day before. Went to work, was told that I would be deducted a dollar from my pay. After speaking to my Captain, he said he would try to fix it up. Got a job at the Supply Room which isn't so bad. Went home at 12:00 and spoke to John Passantino. Said he would make a trunk for me. We started and worked all afternoon. Went to a party that night. Had a nice time. Met a pretty girl. Her name was Terry. She was nice and sociable. Walked her home, then went home and signed off for the night.
P.S. James C. came home from Fort Hancock. Said he liked it there and was going back the next day.

Monday, April 24, 1933

Met boys at station. Arrived at army base as usual. Got our last injection which was another honey. Later started working in Supply giving out sheets. Then went to laundry, worked pretty hard. Felt very bad--had a toothache all that night. Talked to Chris and found

*out it was no dice. John C. came around with car. Rode around, had
some fun with the boys. Went to bed at ten.*

Tuesday, April 25, 1933

*Got up and felt lousy. Wanted to stay home but changed my mind
and came to work. Did a little work in supply room. Had lunch,
went home at four. Got some bad news about Samie. They kept him
at the children's court. Willie Brown came over, stayed at the house
for the night. Not much excitement for one night so I went to bed at
11:00.*

Wednesday, April 26, 1933

*Got up early, arrived at base at 6:45. Listened to another lecture at
morning exercise. Cleaned up supply room, shaved, took a bath and
shower. Later wrote a letter to T. Rom. Got pass from Captain to
stay out for Thursday if I wanted to. Was home for supper. Grace
and Angelo came over for the night. Met John C. Went for ride, got
home early, went to bed.*

Thursday, April 27, 1933

*Got up at 11:00 for first time in weeks and felt lazy all day. Went
down to Child Court in the afternoon about Samie. Couldn't see
him but found out the trial was over Tuesday and he was found
guilty and the verdict was set for next Tues. Got home and called
Mr. Parlatore to see if he could do anything about it. Said he would
come over on the morrow to talk it over. Not much doing that night
so I signed over for the night.*

You boys know how much I love your Uncle Sammy now, but he was such a pain in the ass in 1933 when he was 12. He was always doing stupid stuff, wandering around the neighborhood with his "hoodlum" friends. He cut school a lot and we had visits from several NYC truant officers. Remember that my mom and dad still couldn't speak English very well, so it was up to me and Grace, the oldest children, to handle legal stuff like this. Our lawyer, Anthony Parlatore lived down the block and was trying to keep Sammy out of jail, but this time he was sent to what they called a "Reform School" for juvenile delinquents. It was housed on Randalls Island where he would have to spend 12 months.

He and his best friend, Johnny Ippolito, who everyone called Johnny Boy, were out late one night and they met two guys and two girls from Canarsie who were walking near the train station. Johnny said something to one of the girls and before you knew it, a fight broke out. Now, Sammy and Johnny had gotten into lots of fights, but this time, Johnny took out a pocketknife and stabbed one of the guys in the arm. The girls started yelling, Sammy and Johnny ran, but the cops found them as they were heading back home. Sammy and Johnny were charged with assault. Despite his efforts, Mr. Parlatore could not help Sammy.

I'll never forget the day he had to leave for the reform school. He was sobbing uncontrollably, and so was I and the rest of the family. Grandma was trying to hold onto him as the guard walked him to the police car. As he was getting into the car, he turned and looked at us and continued bawling. My baby brother was going to reform school, and I was getting ready to leave him and the rest of the family to travel to somewhere I didn't even know. I felt so guilty.

The good news was he was released after 8 months and seemed to have grown up. When he and Johnny turned 18, they joined the CCCs and were sent to the Kennesaw Mountain National Battlefield Park in Georgia.

Between the months in reform school and the stint in the CCCs, Sammy had come full circle, and really made me proud. And right after Pearl Harbor in 1941, he and Johnny were among the first to enlist and both earned medals for bravery.

Rule 9
Appreciate the Little Things in Life

Monday, May 1, 1933

Up early and at the Base. The boys got paid. I was the only one not to get paid and was I disappointed. Our squad got changed to different quarters much better than where we were. Worked in Supply room. Later went down to laundry, worked until 4 then got pass. Went home, hung around, went riding, saw Pauline, but did not talk to her. Later went for a walk with the boys, made an appointment this day with the dentist.

I still wasn't getting used to getting up at 5:00, but somehow, I did it again on Friday. At breakfast, we started talking about where the government might be sending us. Since we were the first CCC class, there was no way to know where we would be. The rumor was it would probably be a state park, but that limited the selection to one of the 48 states. Most of the guys said they were hoping to go far away. Jack DeFeo, who thought he was God's gift to women, said he hoped he'd get a free trip to California because he was so handsome, they would discover him and he'd become a movie star. We all laughed. Frankie Scotto said he was tired of the cold weather in Brooklyn and wanted to go to Florida. He had little to say when we reminded him, we would only be away from May to October. And a guy named Bernie wanted to be sent to Chicago so he could see the World's Fair. When it was my turn, I said the only state park I knew was at Bear Mountain, and I could come home on weekends if they sent me there. I got a lot of razzing from the guys because despite my wanderlust, maybe I wasn't adventurous.

Pauline and I were getting along great and I hated the thought of not being able to see her for six months. One night, we headed to Coney Island, one of our favorite spots. Most of the rides had just reopened, and despite the tons of food we were getting at the base, I had a hankering for a couple of Nathan's hot dogs. But the main reason we went was to see Baby Mary. Walking along the boardwalk we passed Steeplechase Park, fortune tellers, games of skill like a shooting gallery and ring toss, and booths selling pizza, popcorn, cotton candy, and egg creams. Then came the Cyclone, the Wonder Wheel, and Luna Park. Just inside the entrance to Luna Park was Mary.

Outside we heard a barker with a megaphone shouting, "Don't forget to see the babies!"

The sign over the building read "Baby Incubators with Living Babies."

Below, another sign read "All the World Loves Babies." Inside were rows of tiny babies, all from the work of Dr. Martin Couney. This was no crazy sideshow. He had real doctors and real nurses looking after the babies. It was his idea that what he called "preemies" could be saved with what he called "incubators." Apparently, he never charged parents for the care he provided.

Mary only weighed 1 pound, 10 ounces when she was born in a hospital in Brooklyn. Most babies who are born so tiny died, but someone at the hospital told her parents about the incubators at Coney Island, and Dr. Couney might be able to help. Mary was growing stronger each day. And Pauline and I had been following her progress for the past three months.

We each paid our 25 cents and down the first row, behind the glass, we saw Mary. She was asleep, but when we tapped on the glass, (which was forbidden) she opened her eyes for a bit. The sign on her incubator said she now weighed three and a half pounds and had been at Coney Island for 72 days. She was surrounded by many more babies, some smaller than Mary and some nearly ready to go home. The building was so clean and well-lit. Several doctors and lots of nurses were moving about, constantly checking on the little ones. In addition to the regular nurse, several wet nurses were feeding the babies.

Pauline and I fell in love with Mary the first time we went to see Dr. Couney's Incubators. We met Mary's mother and father one day, and between their tears and smiles, they told us how lucky they felt to be giving Mary a chance. Her parents were not any older than we were, which gave us a real connection to her and them. Pauline would squeeze my hand tightly whenever we saw Mary and we looked at each other and thought about a child we might have someday.

Pauline and I got off the train and walked to her house. We hugged and kissed, and I noticed that she was crying.

"Don't cry," I said as I hugged her even harder. "I'll only be gone for six months and I will write to you when I can,"

"I know," she said, "but I really love you and want you to stay here so we can make plans. I'm going to be twenty-one in a few weeks, and I was hoping we could think about getting married. So many of my friends are already engaged."

"I love you too. I'm so sorry I am leaving, but it's something I have to do. When I get back, we can get serious and make those plans."

We kissed one final time, and I walked the two blocks to my house. I did love Pauline, but part of me wondered if what I told her about marriage plans would actually happen. Would I still feel the same after six months in the CCCs?

Tuesday May 2, 1933
Arrived at Base at 6:40. Had some trouble in Mess Hall with a tough sergeant. Had to stay in there and help. Later went down for roll call, later worked in supply room then was called to sign roll call. Later got pass to go home, played ball with boys on the corner. I got Info about transferring Jim here at Army Base. Got home at 10:30, went to bed with a terrific toothache. Couldn't sleep all night.

Wednesday May 3, 1933
Got up 1 hour late, arrived late for first time, found someone slept in my bed at Base. Spoke to Captain Hawley, then he wrote to Fort Hancock trying to get Jim sent here. Got my first salary today. Got my tooth pulled out. Didn't hurt much but I was spitting blood all day and that night. Met Anna that night. She gave me a note from Terry about some dance which I hope I could go. Went to bed about 10:30, my gums hurting

Thursday May 4, 1933
I got one of the worst toothaches I ever had in my life. I thought I'd go crazy. I didn't sleep any more that morning until I got to the base and saw M.D.

Friday May 5, 1933
Arrived at base with a toothache, saw the M.D., fixed my tooth, gave me some pills. Went and laid down and felt much better. Listened to Captain warn us about dangers in Woods.

Saturday May 6, 1933: At the Movies
Got up, dressed up, had breakfast, left for Base. It started to rain when I got off train. looked like it was going to be a lousy day. Had an inspection of all bunks and clothes. Later went down to Pier to meet boat that Jim wrote about, but it never came. Dressed up in Civilian clothes, went to meet Pauline. Met her and went to a show & saw "Gabriel Over the White House." Had a nice time, left her late in the afternoon, went home, met Jim and Mary over the house.

The Missing Days

At this point, the book has several blank pages and is missing twenty days. I can only speculate why, after five weeks of diligently writing every day, I stopped writing on May 6th. The blank pages indicate that I meant to fill in those days, but after the blank pages, I left for the West. The major missing entry was when we found out where we would be stationed and when we were to leave. There wasn't much ceremony except for a posting we read on the bulletin board one afternoon. The best news was Jimmy, Mario, and I, and a bunch of other guys we knew would be traveling across the country to Yellowstone Park in Montana and Wyoming. We would be leaving on June 3, and it was then that I picked up my journal and wrote again. The style for the rest of the journal was very different from the previous entries. It is written in red ink, and the dates flow together.

Part Two
New York to Montana

Rule 10

Love Your Country

Saturday, June 3, 1933

Trip from New York to Montana (N.Y. TIME USED ALL THROUGH TRIP)
Left Brooklyn Army Base at 6 p.m. by boat to Weehawken, New Jersey arrived at 7 p.m. Train left at 11:40 p.m. It was by New York Central.

Traveled along Hudson River past Bear Mt. and West Point and Albany at 2:00 a.m. Passed Utica at 5 a.m. Arrived at Syracuse at 8 a.m. Very nice town stopped for a while for water & fuel. On our way again to Rochester arrived at 10 a.m. After having roll call and a little exercise got ready to leave at 11:00 a.m. On our way again passed through the town of Chile at 11:25 then later past the town of South Byron at 11:45 a.m. Went through town of Batavia —a very nice town at 12:05. On our way to Buffalo, we passed through Depew at 12:30 p.m. Arrived at Buffalo at 12:45. A very nice city, quiet and peaceful looking.

Left Buffalo at 1:20 p.m. then went through Derby and Erie PA at 70 miles per hr. and a few other small towns on the outskirts of

*Penn. Then we left Penn, and into Ohio. Arrived at a town called
Painesville after a little engine trouble. Left there at 4:45 p.m. and
was on our way to Cleveland.*

*I had been taking short notes of all the cities I could spot along the
way, towns like Derby, Erie, and Painsville. Our next stop was in
Cleveland where the guys were able to stretch their legs for about a
half-hour before setting off towards Toledo. Back on train again.
Left Cleveland at 6:15 p.m. and passed thru Lindale, a small town
in Ohio. Then we went over Lake Erie, a beautiful sight at 7:30,
then thru some towns, Gypsum,
Danbury, at a terrific speed, arrived at Toledo at 8:15 p.m.*

The first Brooklyn Rule says that young men must not leave
Brooklyn, so even though we would be back, that entire
week was stressful. The night before we left, our group gathered at
the club to say farewell to me, Jimmy and Mario. It was a bit sad
saying goodbye to the guys and ladies, but it felt good to have
such nice friends. Everyone said they would write, and I said I
would write back. Johnny Cala had agreed to drive me Jimmy and
Mario to the base the next day. I got home about midnight.

On the final morning, I got up at 6:00 and had my usual
breakfast—coffee and several of my mother's biscotti. What
followed was much hugging and kissing and holding back tears.
Grace and Fanny warned me about what they called "wild
women." Mama gave me a list of instructions, mostly about eating
and putting on some weight. My father had barely acknowledged
my joining the Corps or the fact that I was leaving. But that
morning, completely out of character, he hugged me tight and
said, *A fattu brava, figlio mio,* which sort of means, "You've done
well, my son." He kissed me and I burst into tears.

J ohnny picked me up around 7:00, and we headed to the base
for the last time. We spent that day packing our belongings,
getting last-minute instructions on our roles in the corps and
how to behave because we represented the corps. I said goodbye to
friends heading to different camps, and those of us heading to
Yellowstone got together. Around 4:00, they served us a terrific
early dinner.

"I think we should call this the Last Supper," said Mario.
"Who wants to play Jesus?"

"I can be Judas," said Jimmy. "Duke, why don't you be
Jesus?"

"I'd much rather be Peter," I said. "He's got a whole basilica
named after him in the Vatican. And wasn't he the favorite of
Jesus?"

After dinner, I thanked many of the men who had trained
and taken care of us on the base. Even though we gave them a
tough time, they prepared us for what awaited us. We were
assigned Camp 1260 and told to get on bus Y24 which would
take us to Weehawken, New Jersey where we would board the NY
Central. The bus made a lot of noise, but the guys were quiet as
we turned left onto Flushing Avenue to begin our great odyssey.
About ten minutes later, we made a right turn and there it was.
The Brooklyn Bridge.

The bridge was a thing of beauty. I had been on it many times,
but this was different. My heart was pounding as we began to
cross it. It stretched out leading away from everything I knew.
Brooklyn was fading fast from my view. I wondered if I'd ever see
this bridge again, if I'd ever taste my mother's cooking or hear the
radio playing in the candy store. A lump rose in my throat.

I looked around at my fellow travelers. Nearly all were trying
to sleep or reading magazines, oblivious to what I was experiencing. I was headed west to Yellowstone to work in the CCCs. A
new life was stretching out before me. It was a long way to

Montana, but for now, I was just a kid on a bus, crossing a bridge into the unknown.

———

We got to New Jersey around 7:00, but our train didn't leave until close to midnight. We would be traveling along the Hudson River to Albany and then turning towards Buffalo and points West.

Our first stop was Cleveland about 5:30 the next night, where we could finally walk around a bit. "Are we having fun yet? Is everyone enjoying Cleveland?" I asked a few guys who were standing near a phone booth and having a smoke.

"I hate this shit, Duke," said Jimmy. "I wish we could at least get to a bar or something, but 30 minutes isn't enough time to do anything."

"Yeah," added Sal Romano, a guy who was in our railroad car. "I wish we could check out the local females in this hick town."

The guys all laughed, seeing the railroad station was huge. "Well, Sal, they do have a baseball team here and lots of tall buildings from what I can see. But if you want to see a real hick town, I bet there will be lots of them in Montana."

"I guess I'm already missing good old Brooklyn," Sal answered. "I'm wondering if this was a good idea." Nobody said anything, probably because most of us were thinking the same thing as we headed back to the train. I told myself that I needed to stop weighing my decision. Dammit, I was going to be all-in.

As the train pulled into Toledo, what I saw made me furious. Besides being a giant, grimy, factory town, I saw several Hoovervilles along the tracks. These shanty towns had popped up all over the country for the homeless and were called "Hoovervilles." When the train slowed down, we passed less than 50 feet from one of these makeshift camps. I saw a sea of sad, desperate-looking people, crippled old men, teenage kids in rags, frail women holding babies, and a separate smaller group of Black people. It was clear even these camps were segregated. Some of those closest to the train were staring at us, and one young, emaciated woman made eye contact with me. I had to look away.

As the train sped up, I couldn't get those poor, miserable people off my mind, and I thought back to the trip me and my pals took to see the Tin City camp in Brooklyn back in April. That trip really frightened me.

I had read an article in the *Brooklyn Eagle* back in December, "Tin City" Folks Gird For Dreariest Winter." The subhead said, "One Meal a Day Is the Average Fare of Denizens Who Miss Wood for Their Home-Made Stoves." As I read this, I realized this "Hooverville" was in nearby Red Hook and was the home of 500 unemployed men and their families. These guys were merchant seamen, most from Norway and Sweden, who came to Brooklyn as sailors on some of the merchant ships docked in Red Hook. When the Depression hit, and those merchant ships were no longer sailing, these guys were left in a foreign country with no way to go home. The term "Tin City" referred to the shacks many of them had constructed out of tin cans. That article stuck in my head for months, and then, a recent article said there were now over 1,000 people there. Since I already knew I would be joining the CCCs next month, I really wanted to see what the Depression was actually doing to some folks. Sure, our family was struggling to make ends meet, and my father and mother were on Relief, but we each had a bed to sleep in and some food to eat. From what I had been reading, Tin City was the worst place to be.

So, one Saturday afternoon in April, I asked Jimmy, Charlie Cala, Joe Rocco, and Sammy Stone if they wanted to go see Tin City. Joe Rox said he would drive and soon we were off in his '29 Chevy.

"Seeing this will be good for laughs," said Charlie.

"I'm not so sure it will be funny," I said. "How can we make fun of these people?"

As soon as we arrived, everyone got quiet. The first thing that hit us as we got out of the car was the smell. It's hard to describe, but it was a smell I'll never forget. It was a combination of death, decay, and sickness. Spread out before us were acres and acres of humanity. It was almost too much to take in. The inhabitants were mostly men, but we did see some women and children. The shacks were thrown together with a variety of junk, and it seemed like they were ready to collapse if a strong breeze were to come. We walked through part of the place, listening to some of them speaking in a foreign language, and we felt like somehow, we were intruding on their misery. Most of the people looked lost, and I felt we had become voyeurs.

"Let's the hell out of here," I said. "This place is horrible."

"Jesus, I never imagined anything so terrible," said Joe. "I'm sorry I said going there would be good for a laugh."

None of us replied, and as we were heading back to the car, no one spoke. Standing next to Joe's car on Sigourney Street was a wisp of a man with a scraggly beard. His dirty gray trousers were held up with a piece of rope, and his brown shirt was torn and filthy. He held out his skinny hand hoping to get some money from us. We each dug into our pockets and gave him whatever change we had.

Then, as if the money triggered something in him, he started talking nonstop. "What did you boys think about our little dump," he said in English with a strong Scandinavian accent.

"It's really an awful place. How did you and all these people end up here?" I asked.

"There are no ships heading back to my wife and children in Norway. My name is Chris Lavold."

"So what do you guys do here now, Chris?" said Jimmy. "How do you spend your days"

"I spend each morning trying to get a little work, but it is mostly a waste of time." He looked like an old man, so it shocked us when he told us he was 35.

"No fresh water or toilets here," he said. "Each day I have to haul drinking water from a public pump several blocks away on Dykeman Street. Me and a few other guys scrounge for firewood from nearby buildings and trash heaps."

"How do you get food?"

"Some men used to fish from the docks, but the water had gotten too disgusting, even for the fish."

"Then what do you eat?" I asked again.

"I tried to grow some vegetables like corn and tomatoes, but the dirt was pretty polluted as well. I usually go to the Norwegian Seamen's Church or the Salvation Army for something to eat." Then he pointed to an area to the far left and said the people there were mostly Porto Ricans. "We were newcomers," he said. "And some regulars resented them for competing for firewood or even some possible work, even though they were here first."

"Too bad," said Charlie. "I can't imagine living like this. How do you do it?"

"Lots of the men had died during the winter, and some had even gone blind after drinking some homemade alcohol."

But he got excited just a bit when he told us a baby had been born on March 23. I looked at the other guys and wondered what fate was in store for that innocent child. As we pulled out, he gave us a weak wave and a half smile. On the ride back, Sammy Stone made fun of Chris, and we all told him to shut up.

A fter that day, I knew my decision to join the CCCs was the right one. The opportunity to earn a dollar a day and get three square meals while people like Chris were out begging for food was smart. And from the other changes President Roosevelt had been making, it looked like maybe horrors like we had just witnessed might be fixed soon.

But this camp in Toledo was so much larger than our Tin City back in New York. As far as I could see, it was a sea of broken-down shanties made with wood from crates, cardboard, scraps of metal, or whatever materials these homeless folks could find. Several stray dogs were looking for something to eat, and a group of men were waiting in line for food. I felt guilty because I still had half of a baloney sandwich in my jacket pocket.

I know it's weird, but I couldn't get a popular song out of my head.

In a Shanty in Old Shanty Town

It's only a shanty
In old Shanty Town
The roof is so slanty

It touches the ground
But my tumbled down shack
By the old railroad track
Like a millionaire's mansion
Is calling me back

I'd give up a palace
If I were a king
It's more than a palace
It's my everything

There's a Queen waiting there
With a silvery crown
In a shanty in old Shanty Town

Rule 11
Embrace Your Culture

We left Toledo at 9:05. Rode along pretty fast through Delta then thru Wauseum at 10 p.m. Then into the state of Indiana—a very beautiful state. Arrived at Elkhart at 10:05 p.m. a lively city. Apparently, the people knew we were coming and the large crowd had formed at the station. We had a few minutes to speak to some folks who were very sociable. Left there at 11:40 on our way again at a rapid pace.

Arrived in Chicago at 12:35 on N.Y. time which was 2 hrs. different already. Only the few of us who were in charge of cars were awake,. Stopped for a few hrs. took a walk, saw some of the "World's Fair" but couldn't stay very long. But what we saw was very pretty, all lit up like Luna Park only much nicer.

Left Chicago at 3:55 then went to bed and couldn't see where we went through. The Pullman train was swell. I had a compartment for myself as I was in charge of the car.

It had been a long day, so most of the guys on the train were asleep. After another quick stop in Elkhart, Indiana, the train got to Chicago about 12:30, which was only 10:30 Central time.

Like most of the guys on the train, Jimmy and Mario were fast asleep.

But I shook them both and said, "You are not going to believe this!" Jimmy just grumbled.

"Let me sleep,' said Mario. "You are such a pain in the ass."

"I might be, but look outside the window on the right."

"Holy shit," Mario said. "It looks like Luna Park! Where are we?"

"It's Chicago, and it's the World's freaking Fair. And the sarge said we have a three-hour layover."

"Let's go," he said. "Get up, Jimmy!"

Most of the guys stayed on the train to sleep and were going to miss a great opportunity. As the three of us stepped off, the conductor said, "This is the 23rd Street entrance to the World's Fair. We'll be here until 2:30, so you boys better be back in time. But have some fun!"

What we saw was amazing. As far as we could see, the sky was filled with light, bright, brilliant light, in all directions. Mario repeated that it reminded him of Luna Park in Coney Island, and we agreed. Entering the Fair, we passed by the rustic Belgian Village and the huge Firestone Building before stopping at the General Cigar Company pavilion.

"Hey, maybe we can get us some free smokes, let's check it out." We watched some old guy rolling cigars and explaining how they were made, but we were mostly interested in the free cigars we hoped he would hand out when he finished.

He went on saying, "This machine behind me can produce 10,000 cigars a day and the machine on the right adds the wrappers. It's all done without being touched by a human hand. That's what we call progress."

After lighting our White Owls, we wandered towards "The Streets of Paris" exhibit, right next to Lake Michigan. It had a miniature Eiffel Tower and was all lit up. It looked really fine, and we were headed there when Mario saw a sign directing them to the Italian Village.

"Forget about Belgium and Paris," said Jimmy. "Let's go to Italy!"

We were not disappointed because, after a long ride in a cramped train, what we saw was exactly what we needed. Outside were several large bronze sculptures, replicas I think of some famous ones in Italy. We found a large bazaar which reminded me of the Saint Fortunata feast. The smells were familiar and incredible. There were booths displaying products from various Italian provinces. Our first stop was at an exhibit of Italian wine from all over Italy. Without even speaking to each other, we went straight to the Sicily section. There was a gorgeous redhead pouring small glasses, saying stuff about the aroma and hints of this and how this one was from the Mount Etna region in Sicily and one was from someplace else, but to me both just tasted so smooth, nothing like the wine my Uncle Vincent makes in his basement. The girl was so sweet and sounded like she just got off the boat, so Jimmy was busy flirting and trying to pick her up. I had to remind him our train was leaving in about two hours before we could get him to leave.

Next, we went to a huge tent and got sausage and pepper heroes and beers. We sat at an outside table with a red, white, and green umbrella. An orchestra was playing familiar songs like "*C'è la luna mezzo mare*" and "*Funiculì, Funiculà*," and lots of people were having a good time dancing. I couldn't wait to write to Pauline and tell her about this place. Now I really felt like I was back in Brooklyn, and I wished Pauline was with me.

As we entered the main Italy building, we walked past an enormous portrait of *Il Duce*, Benito Mussolini. Inside were lots of photos of famous and not-so-famous Italians, like Marconi and Volta as well as drawings of people like Marco Polo and Christopher Columbus. On the lower level was a beautiful 20-foot model of the ocean liner, *Rex*. Next to it was a miniature Roman city, and a group of ten Venetian glass blowers doing demonstrations. But time was running out, so we left and headed back.

On the way, we saw more "authentic" villages, from Germany,

Spain, Tunisia, and even an Old English Village. The sounds and smells of all these places were amazing. We walked towards the Pabst Blue Ribbon Casino figuring we could get a quick sample beer for the road and passed the "Streets of Paris" again with only one hour before the train pulled out.

But past the Paris place, I saw a familiar sign about 100 feet away. It said, "Living Babies in Incubators." I let out a yell. "Holy Shit! It's the guy I told you all about. I want to get closer to it now. You guys should head back to the train."

This baby building was immense compared to the one on Coney Island. There was a long line for people to go in, and I realized I was running out of time. Of course, it reminded me of my talk with Pauline and baby Mary back on the Coney Island Boardwalk. I wondered how Mary was doing, and I hoped Pauline would still visit her.

I was looking for a clock, but the only thing around the baby place was a 21-story thermometer sponsored by Havoline Oil. It registered 78 degrees. We left Chicago at 3:55, then I went to bed and couldn't see where we went through. The Pullman train was swell. I had a fine compartment for myself as I was in charge of the car. The boys hated me for that.

Rule 12
Be True to Yourself

Monday, June 5, 1933

Had a nice night's rest. Woke up at 9:30. Rode along arrived at La Crosse, Wisconsin at 10 a.m. A wonderful looking city. We were off again, then we spied the Muddy Mississippi and rode along its banks. Arrived at Overlap, Wis. at 10:30. Indulged in some calisthenics for 20 minutes. People were very nice there. Left Overlap at 11:20 on our way again. Went through town of Analaska at 11:35. Riding along the Mississippi again at a lively rate of speed to St. Paul, Minnesota. Arrived there at 2:00 p.m. There we were told to stretch our legs for a while. St. Paul is a very large and pretty city. Our train was refueled and at 3:00 p.m. we were on our way again and went thru a bunch of small towns which I didn't notice as I was playing cards and sleeping—my usual afternoon nap.
We were going over the Detroit Lake when I awoke. A nice lake which is along the Minn. border. We crossed the border and into the state of North Dakota at 8:30 p.m. A large city with a population of 30,000 called Fargo. We stopped, had some eats, and looked the place over. Meanwhile, our train changed engines, and we were ready to leave at 10 p.m.

Went through town called Castleton which was still in North Dakota at 10:40 p.m. Then I signed off for the night and couldn't keep track of the other cities we passed during the night.

Tuesday, June 6, 1933: Into Montana

Woke up still in N. Dakota. Had breakfast, cleaned up myself and sat at the window as we passed the state line into Montana at 10:10 A.M. We then saw mountains for the first time all day. We rode thru deserts and not many towns. We stopped at some small water tank for half an hour and refueled and were off to some town called Bull Mt. A nice quiet town at 8:45 that evening. Rolling off again through Osbourne Mont. like a flash.

Our next stop was in a nice big town called Billings. We saw some real cowboys at the station. Some of them were talking to us and trying to discourage us from the woods saying it would kill us to work there. But we kidded them right back. When we got started, some of the cowboys gave us a reception and were riding along with the train on their horses and hollering like Indians while we laughed ourselves sick at them.

The train was going along pretty fast for a few hours till we came to a Wonderful town called Livingston which I'll never forget as long as I live. The train stopped for the night. They gave some of us leave until 5 a.m. and then the fun began. We first visited a saloon just like in the movies: a long bar with sawdust on the floor and gambling tables. This was the first time I started to realize I was really in the West. I gave the man behind the bar a $5 bill and he gave me change in Silver Dollars. Then we went to a section of town called B Street and there I saw things I never saw before, which I can't explain in this book. Then we went to the Cafeteria for a bite to eat and I met the sweetest girl in the West. Her name was Marie Grasse. She was very nice and pleasant to talk to. She got stuck on my style, so I walked out with her and learned she was stopping at the Northern Hotel in Livingston. I went up to her suite (two rooms) and had a very nice time, almost missed my train which left at 5:15.

On June 6, 1933, I wrote I would never forget what I experienced in Livingston, Montana, "as long as I live." I mentioned that to you at the start of this book. And I was right. So much is still vivid 30 years later, especially because it was the day I lost my virginity, and I came of age.

But my transformation began with something trivial earlier, when we had a quick stop in Billings. Most of the folks we had been meeting along our journey pretty much looked and dressed and spoke like us, and were dealing in various ways with the Depression. But meeting those real-life cowboys signaled something different, as if we had arrived at a new country, one as far away from Brooklyn and the Depression as could be. Some of those guys we met were probably about my age, and yet my sense was their lives were nothing like mine. They were real-life ranchers. Talking with a group of them at the station gave me the sense they were innocent and free in a way I wasn't. Just watching them waving their hats and yelling as they followed along with our train was exhilarating. As the train moved along, I realized my first 19 years were frozen in the past, and I was about to become a man and think differently, a man who might not obey the Brooklyn Rules.

Then we stopped at Livingston, an unforgettable place. As I write this, I realized the word "living" in the town's name has had special meaning to me, as I truly felt alive after Livingston. We arrived early in the afternoon, and Jimmy and Mario and I spotted a place with a crooked sign with the name "The Living Stone Saloon."

As soon as we entered, Jimmy said, "Holy shit! Is this a movie set?" Mario and I laughed because we all had seen so many Western movies. My favorites were those with Hoot Gibson, Ken Maynard, Harry Carey, and Gabby Hayes. I think most of those pictures had a barroom scene, and this one looked just like those places. It was dark and dusty and it had sawdust all over the floor.

Over the bar were stuffed elk and bear heads. Everyone had a hat on—some black, some tan, some white—and many were wearing bandanas. A few women dressed in jeans just like the cowboys were sitting at some tables, but we also saw some women in frilly dresses. And, of course, like any Western movie, someone was playing a honky-tonk piano.

Mario looked at the two of us and said," OK, pardners, let's have some whiskey."

We walked past a table with four scruffy old guys playing cards with a bottle on the table and headed to the bar.

"Three whiskeys," we said in unison.

Trying to act like this was normal, we downed those shots together and smashed our glasses onto the bar. The whiskey was more powerful than any of us expected, and the bartender had a broad grin.

"Want another round, boys?"

"I think maybe I'll just have a beer," I said.

The guys chimed in with the same. We stayed for a while, and the bartender told us we should check out B Street while we were in town. When I put a $5 bill on the bar, he gave me another four silver dollars change. Welcome to the West.

What I witnessed on B Street was like nothing I had ever seen. I tried to be vague about it in my journal but I can tell you more now. As we turned onto the street, there were ten pretty houses but as we got closer, there were women in the open windows in every house or on the porches inviting us to come in.

"Five dollars for a quick one," one of them said. We nodded and walked on.

Other women offered a variety of sexual acts in such crude and explicit language that it actually embarrassed me. There were women much younger than me, very old women, fat women, tiny women, Black women, and Indian women. A few houses had young children playing in the yards. These women were dressed in elaborate outfits, mostly skimpy, and many showing off their breasts. The three of us kept walking slowly down the block, despite getting lewd invitations. At one, there was a piano playing, at several we smelled marijuana in the air, at one we actually saw a woman giving a man oral sex right on the open porch. We could see many of our CCC recruits taking advantage of these women, but somehow, the three of us kept walking and went to get some food.

Looking back, it was the right decision, but I have to admit seeing all that sex up close had really got me excited. We got back to the center of town and headed right to a nice place simply called "Cafeteria." It was clean and well-lit and served a tremendous variety of food, including elk, bison, and even bear meat. We each grabbed a tray and walked through the line, selecting food we were familiar with. Mario had meatloaf and mashed potatoes, Jimmy, a cheeseburger with fries, and I, pork chops with buttered noodles. We noticed two pretty girls at one table, so we sat across from them and introduced ourselves.

"Hello," said Mario. "This is Jimmy and this is Mike, though we call him Duke."

"Howdy," the blonde said. "My name is Sandy, and this here is Jane. We work over at the bakery down the block."

Jimmy started talking them up, and I watched him put on the charm. I had seen this act before, but Sandy and Jane seemed to eat it up. Across the table, I saw this beautiful redhead sitting alone. When I caught her eye, she smiled and gave me a little wave. I waved back, said goodbye to my pals and their girls, and moved to that table.

As I was about to sit down, she said, "I'm Marie. I'm not from here, and it looks like you and your friends aren't locals either."

"You're right. Me and them are headed to Yellowstone with the CCCs. We just got a break from our train. And my name is Mike."

The conversation continued. I told her I was from Brooklyn; she said she was originally from San Francisco and she worked for a hotel chain. We talked and soon I realized Jimmy and Mario and their new friends were gone.

We walked outside and found a bench and kept talking. "I really like your style," she said. "By the way, my last name is Grasse."

"Is that Italian?" I asked.

"Sure thing. My mother and father were both born in Naples, and settled out West in 1905. I was born in Sacramento, but we then moved to Frisco. My dad works for General Electric, and he's in charge of converting and maintaining all the old steam-powered cable cars to electricity."

I told her my parents had come from Sicily, and my dad had lost his job at Bloomingdales, and she reached out and held my hand and said, "I'm sorry."

I couldn't believe how beautiful she was, and then she said something I wasn't prepared for.

"I work for the Borden Hotel in Bozeman, and they sent me to Livingston to check out the Northern Hotel here. The owners are thinking of buying it, so I am to secretly look it over and tell them if it's worth it. I have a lovely two-room suite there and I'd hate to spend the night alone."

I didn't know what to say.

Before I knew it, we were walking hand-in-hand, on our way to what proved to be an amazing night.

"Wait here in the lobby," she said. "Then in about 10 minutes, take the elevator up to the third floor. I'm in room 321."

The hotel actually had an elevator! The lobby was luxurious, filled with red velvet chairs and sofas. I'll admit I was nervous sitting and waiting for the 10 minutes which seemed like an hour. I went to her room and what followed was a night of ecstasy. The suite was gorgeous. She had already changed into a flimsy black negligee and greeted me with our first kiss. She looked stunning. How odd was it! We were about to spend the night together and hadn't even kissed until then.

"I ordered a bottle of Champagne," she said. "Crack it open and we'll have a toast."

In addition to the Champagne, she had ordered some tasty appetizers from room service. I poured out two glasses and we clinked our glasses. The setting was perfect. But I felt far from perfect, having been on trains for several days. "I desperately need a shower," I said. "Don't go anywhere." She laughed and I excused myself. The bathroom was all done in green and blue marble. I was feeling like a big shot, not like a simple 19-year-old from Brooklyn. I could have showered forever were it not for who was waiting for me.

The sex was so much better than I could have imagined. I think Marie knew it was my first time, so she was gentle and wonderful. I had lots of experience with girls, but most of it was what we used to call "petting." This was a night I had only dreamed about.

I was so glad my first time was with someone I really liked, as opposed to those women on B Street.

And the funny thing was, during the entire night, I had no thoughts of Pauline. Or of Brooklyn. Or of those damn rules.

I woke up at about 4:30 and remembered our train was leaving at 5:00.

"Holy shit!" I said. "I hate to make love and leave, but I have a train to catch." Marie laughed and asked for my address and gave me hers and assured me we would see each other again. The Northern Hotel was right across from the railroad station, but I barely made it in time.

"Well, the lover boy decided to join us," said Mario. "We thought you and that floozie ran off and eloped."

"Very funny. How did you and Jimmy make out after I saw you?"

"Never mind us," said Jimmy. "We want to know all the details about your night of carnal bliss. C'mon, tell us about your fancy fornicating and all your shaking of the sheets."

I said nothing. I just grinned. I was so happy to have had the experience that I couldn't find words to express it, and I wouldn't have said anything to them if I could. I kept thinking about it for days, weeks, and even months afterward. Even now, 30 years later, it still makes me happy to think about that magical night with Marie Grasse.

Part Three
Yellowstone
Expect the Unexpected

Rule 13
Enjoy What Nature Gives Us

Wednesday June 7, 1933, Yellowstone--Day 1

On our way again after a night of Surprises and wonderful experiences. After riding for a few hours thru plenty of mountains with 2 engines pulling our train, we finally arrived at Gardiner, the North Gate to Yellowstone Park. The town was very small but nice. We unloaded the trains, got on trucks and we started for the Camp. We rode up mountains like I never seen before, valleys, cliffs, canyons, falls, volcanoes, everything was very pretty. Every once in a while, we would see a bear or elk and many other animals. Everything was new to us. Then we passed the Grand Canyon and stopped for a break. I stood amazed at first. It was so deep and the rock was all colored and there were large water falls twice as high as Niagara Falls. We were on our way again up the mountains. The higher we got, the colder it got. We almost froze before we reached the camp, which was 54 miles away from the North Gate. What a hike. Everything seemed pretty tough the first day. The eats were not ready and everybody was disgusted.

There was plenty of snow all around the place. It was cold at night. The next day we were still disgusted, but after walking around and looking the place over, I changed my mind and made up my mind

*to like the place and I certainly liked it after that. Most of my
friends were always crying. They wanted to go home and they never
were satisfied until they got sent home and it was a pleasure to get
rid of them.*

Our incredible cross-country journey ended when we
arrived at Gardiner, Montana, a tough little frontier town.
At this point in my journal, I just stopped including dates, probably because I was so exhausted each night. I would only write
about once a week, usually on Saturday or Sunday, and I tried to
include as much of what had been happening. I also wrote letters
home, and I guess my sister had kept them because they were in
my footlocker along with the letters from home and friends I had
kept.

We had to switch trains several times, but this last train
comprised five passenger cars being pulled by two huge locomo-
tives which held 40 guys in each car. Each troop would go to a
different campsite.

Once we unloaded all of our gear, we were told to line up in
front of the train cars because some bureaucrats wanted to get a
photograph of the entire trainload. We were making history, they
told us, and they wanted to document it. So, 200 tired boys had to
stand at attention while some guy standing on a ladder 100 feet
away took the photo.

Then I met the Sarge.

"This is the sorriest assemblage of humans I've ever seen,"
yelled this old guy, who we later learned was Sergeant John
Rosasco.

He was short with a huge beer belly and several tattoos on his
arm. But I thought it odd that he was carrying something that
looked like a baseball bat, though it was not as long. So, it was
more like a club. What he was looking at was a motley group of
wide-eyed Brooklyn kids, all of whom needed a shower and shave.

We looked disheveled and were wearing an assortment of army surplus supply gear.

"Who's in charge of this mess?" Sarge hollered.

"I think I am," I said. "I have the manifest of our names and contact information, and I was told to give it to the guy who picked us up."

"Give me that list," said Rosasco as he grabbed it from my hand. "And I am not a 'guy.' You will all call me Sergeant Rosasco. Am I clear? And what is your name, young man?"

After I told him my name and nickname, we all followed the sarge to several rickety old trucks and were told to climb into the back. "You are with me in the front, Duke," Sarge said. I didn't know if this was a bad or good thing.

We managed to get all of us along with our gear onto our rusty truck for the long haul to our camp. As we left Gardiner, we saw the Roosevelt Arch, dedicated by President Theodore Roosevelt in 1903, with the inscription, "For the Benefit and Enjoyment of the People." As we drove through the gate, I heard a loud whoop from the guys in the back. We were finally in Yellowstone. I was intimidated by Rosasco, so I acted nonchalant, but I was ready to burst with excitement. After all that training, all those lectures, all that commuting from home to the base, and after all my doubts and fears, I was in Yellowstone.

After a few dusty miles without saying anything, the Sarge spoke. He said he was waiting for hours at the Gardiner railroad station and was pissed off by the time we finally got there.

"As one of the foremen for you goddamn CCC recruits, this is a new experience for me, but it's gonna be easy as shit compared to that goddamn war." (He used the word "goddamn" in nearly every sentence, not just on that day, but as long as he led us.)

"I still have scars from the goddamn Battle of the Argonne Forest in October of '18. I was in the 23rd Infantry, 2nd Division, under General 'Black Jack' Pershing. We lost over 100,000 GIs in that campaign, including so many buddies in our troop. It was goddamn awful."

I was only five when the war ended and I had never really talked to a veteran about it, so I listened and occasionally added words like "wow" or "sorry" or "damn" to what he was telling me. After his war stories, he told me that he had gotten married, had a young son, and his wife divorced him and took the boy. Then he was silent. And he stayed silent for a long time. Of course, he never asked anything about me. I was never clear about why he opened up to me about his personal life that day.

After a long, uncomfortable trip, we arrived at our campsite near the Yellowstone River. It was already dark, so I didn't get to see what it was like. We met Captain Byron Collins when we got off the trucks, and he gave us a quick welcome and told us where we could get some sandwiches and where we would be sleeping. Jimmy, Mario, and I grabbed some grub and headed to this giant tent. We took the first bunks we found and went right to bed. It had been the longest day of my life.

That first morning, I awoke at 5:00, crept out of our tent, and realized I was alone. The sun was rising over the mountains, and I was over 2,000 miles from Brooklyn at an elevation of over 2,000 feet above sea level. "Oh! My! God!" I whispered into the crisp wind on that first day. I had no idea any place could be so beautiful! I filled my lungs with fresh air, unlike the smells and fumes I breathed in every day on Pine Street.

I walked about 50 yards to the center of the field, took another long, deep breath, and tasted more unreal air. It felt like a part of heaven. About 200 feet to my left, I saw a herd of bison looking majestic while grazing undisturbed. I had seen bison in the movies, but not like these beautiful, peaceful giants. To my right, I heard the gentle sound of the river and saw a group of elk wading at the water's edge. The males had the most magnificent antlers that glistened in the rising sun. As I looked off a mile in front of me, I saw towering snow-capped mountains. Then some sounds broke the silence. I heard the distant howl of a wolfpack and the honking of a flock of geese flying overhead.

From our riverside campsite, instead of bricks and concrete

back home, I saw mountains and trees; instead of mice and rats, I saw mountain goats and bald eagles; and instead of man-hole covers and sewers, I saw rivers, lakes, and waterfalls. I never expected to feel this way. Behind me was a huge complex of large brown army tents, one of which was where I had spent the night with another 20 guys. I wanted to take everything in as if this was a sight belonging to me alone. I felt a sense of peace.

Soon a few others joined me, even though they told us Reveille would be at 6:00.

"What the hell are you doing here by yourself?" Jimmy asked. "I got up to take a piss, and I saw your bunk was empty. What gives, Duke?"

"Jimmy, look around you," I said. "Isn't this place awesome? Have you ever imagined it would be this amazing? And this air is so wonderful."

"I mean, it's only a river and some deer and a few buffaloes."

"OK, first of all, those buffaloes are called bison," I said, pointing to the herd that had still not moved from their grazing. "And those deer are actually elk. But look at those majestic mountains, right here where we are living!"

"We saw lots of mountains for the past several hundred miles on the train. But remember, Duke, you're the poet in the group. Me and the other guys back home always thought you were weird because you were always reading books and writing stuff. But damn. I'm hungry now, so enough of your bullshit about the freakin' scenery."

Jimmy was right. I am sort of a romantic for anything beautiful, whether it be a flower growing amid some weeds, a line from a Shakespeare sonnet, or a tiny bird. I guess that was the reason I had started my journal. But Yellowstone was nothing like I had ever witnessed.

Then Mario joined us. He was a lot more impressed about our surroundings than Jimmy was. As Jimmy headed off to the tent, Mario and I drank everything in.

The camp wasn't totally ready for us. A crew of guys—all

locals—had been hired to build real bunkhouses and a mess hall. They were hammering and sawing and cursing all day. We were assigned temporary bunks in these huge tents, and we ate in a smaller tent. And we learned the full contingent of leaders was still on their way, so we had several rather peaceful days.

I was so amazed at my experiences each day in this new land, but I was exhausted each night. I felt scared of what might happen next, but happy to find out. I was depressed about leaving my friends and family, but elated at making new friends and having new adventures; defeated when I could not complete a task, but triumphant when I was able to master one—the first week of CCC camp for me and the boys from Brooklyn was filled with so many improbable ups and downs, it made our heads spin. For the first seven days, we were living in makeshift tents in a world we could never have imagined. And we were going from morning to night in ways I had never done before.

But before we knew it, the workers, supported by a crew of CCC recruits, finished building the Mess Hall and the Recreation Hall. A few weeks later, they finished the bunkhouse. And we were starting to look like a real camp.

The Rec Hall was especially welcome. Prior to its opening, we'd used one of the makeshift tents. It had a ping-pong table, some card tables, chess and checkerboards, and some magazines and newspapers.

M y first attempt at writing a letter home was a failure because I had too much to say and didn't know where to begin. Finally, I wrote a long one:

June 19, 1933

Dear family,

I am good and I hope you all are good too. I hope Sammy is doing OK in reform school, and that Larry is feeling better. Is Grace still working? Has Fanny found a job yet? I hope you are getting the government checks okay.

It took us 4 long days to get here, but it looks like it will be worth it. We stopped in Chicago and me and the boys got to go to the World's Fair for a few hours. What a surprise that was, and we even got to go to the Italian Pavilion for a while.

After riding many hours thru plenty of mountains with 2 engines pulling our train, we finally arrived at the Gardiner, Montana train station on June 7. The town was very small, but nice. We unloaded the trains, met our sarge, got in several big trucks, and entered the North Gate to Yellowstone Park. The gate was an arch made of giant rocks with some words on top, "For the Benefit and Enjoyment of the People."

Our trucks drove right thru it, and then we rode up mountains like I had never seen before, valleys, cliffs, canyons, falls, volcanoes, everything was beautiful. Every once in a while, we saw a bear or elk and many other animals. Everything was new to us. Then we stopped at the Yellowstone Grand Canyon. I stood amazed at first. It was so deep and the rock was all colored and there were large waterfalls twice as high as Niagara Falls. On our way again up the mountains, the higher we got, the colder it got. We almost froze before we reached the camp, which was 54 miles away from the North Gate. What a hike! Everything seemed pretty tough the first day. The eats were not ready and the boys were so angry.

There was plenty of snow all around the place. It was cold at night in our old tents from the war. Sometimes I had to use 2 blankets to keep warm. The next day we were still disgusted, but after walking around and looking the place over, I changed my mind and decided to like the place. Most of the troops were always crying. They wanted to go home and they never were satisfied until they got sent home and it was a pleasure to get rid of them.

Larry, I hope that you are feeling better and the doctor's diagnosis is a good one, I don't know much about tuberculosis, but I'm sure you will get better soon. Please keep your eyes out for Sammy. I do hope he stays out of trouble at the reform school.

Grace, I told some girl that you worked at the Empire State Building, and she was so impressed. Are you still enjoying your job? Have you seen any famous people touring the place?

The food here is pretty good. You know I normally ate a few biscotti and a cup of coffee for breakfast, but here we get the full treatment. Some days, we get stewed prunes, bacon and eggs with a side of toast and hashbrown potatoes. On other days, we get fruit along with pancakes with a side of ham and eggs, either fried or scrambled, and sometimes they even give us omelets. There is also cold cereal and milk if you want it. If we are out in the field for lunch, they bring us a variety of sandwiches and fruit. We get meat at every dinner, whether it's sirloin steak or fried chicken or huge pork chops, or tasty lamb chops along with lots of vegetables and fresh rolls. And, of course, delicious pies and cakes for dessert. On Sundays, we get a roast, either beef or pork or baked ham or lamb, usually with delicious mashed potatoes, salad, and a variety of fruit pies. And with all of our meals, seconds are always available.

Of course, I do miss Mama's cooking, especially on Sundays. Now that you have my address, please send some packages of things like biscotti, salami, pepperoni, cheeses, and even some tomato sauce. I've gotten to know some of the cooks and they might be able to make us Sunday gravy.

Please keep writing. I look forward to the mail each day.

Love Mike

Rule 14
Be Mindful of Your Appearance

June 1933

We went walking around and exploring the mountains, the small tourist camps, and the campfire meetings the rangers gave every night. They had entertainment and lectures every night and all the tourists came and they were very sociable and we got along very nicely with them, especially one girl I met at the lake whose name was Sally. She came from Idaho and I had plenty of fun with her. We started to go out to work at last but we never did much work. We went swimming instead of working and nobody knew the difference.

One day, some of the fellows put up a squawk about food and they started a riot. The rangers were called out. About 25 men from Camp 1259 in Gardiner came in two trucks. They were armed with clubs in case of more trouble. Ten of the ringleaders who started the trouble were put on trucks under guard and were taken to Livingston. I was on the truck to see the boys got to town all right and we had a motorcycle Police escort and what a trip it was.

I was in town all that afternoon until 11 that night. I saw some of the girls I knew from my first visit to that town and I saw Marie and found out she was going back to her hometown but said she would write. That night, coming back to the camp I was nearly frozen to death until we got back there.

As I already mentioned, I stopped using dates in my journal once camp started. My days were filled with planting seedlings, clearing brush for hiking paths, digging trenches, and building dams in the river, and I was either exhausted or busy having new adventures to write daily posts. Most of what you will see here was written on weekends.

The food riot was really funny and had started to brew on the first few days in camp. Many of the "real" Italian kids were not used to basic meat and potato-style meals, and they weren't afraid to say so. No matter what they served us, and in retrospect, it was pretty good food, these guys kept looking for the gravy and macaroni, sausage and peppers, lasagna, chicken parmesan, or ravioli their mothers had been serving them back home. They complained loudly, "We want macaroni! We want macaroni!" Fried chicken, grilled steak, lamb, and pork chops, all with sides of fresh vegetables, rice, noodles, or roasted or mashed potatoes, simply didn't cut it for them.

One Friday night, all hell broke loose. A small group started banging on their metal cups with their spoons, chanting, "We want macaroni!" Suddenly, a guy named Gino threw his baked potato at a friend named Fredo at the next table. Fredo threw it back, but missed Gino and hit the guy next to him. Before we knew it, they were pelting each other and anyone who seemed in charge with bread and whatever else was on their plates, including their plates and glasses. A few other guys at different tables then joined in. The mess hall was in chaos, or should I say "a mess." There was food flying everywhere, and the rest of us were laughing our asses off. Me and my friends scarfed down our food and headed back to our bunks. We could still hear the ruckus until two truckloads of rangers from a nearby camp arrived armed with clubs and guns and began "breaking heads." Everybody gathered outside the building to see what would happen next. The ten ringleaders were rounded up, handcuffed, and placed in a separate tent under guard for the night. We were in shock as we watched them being led away. But later, the rangers had a sense of humor and stood by with their rifles out while the ringleaders had to clean up the mess.

The next morning, Captain Collins assigned me to go with Jack, one of the staff guys in the truck to Livingston to send these guys home along with some form of punishment. The CCCs were not like the army—one could leave at any time, though the monthly payments home would immediately stop, so I never found out what form of punishment those troublemakers got.

So about 10:00, me and Jack and one of the Rangers named Pete set out for the Livingston RR station. It was pretty great being a leader, especially because I could spend the whole day in my beloved Livingston, looking for my sweet Marie. Our truck took us right to the local sheriff's office. There Pete and Jack were taking these guys to a holding pen when one of them tried to run off. I stood and watched, as the sheriff, Jack, and Pete got him back. It was pretty exciting.

After I was "relieved from duty," Jack said we would stay in Livingston until 11:00 PM. He didn't say why, but I had the impression he was headed to B Street for a bit of pleasure. Pete was going to stay with the troublemakers overnight. I went back to the cafeteria and had a nice dinner and saw Sandy and Jane, the girls Jimmy and Mario had "connected" with. We chatted for a long while, and then I spotted Marie walking in. I stood up and walked right over to her.

"Hello, Michael. Fancy meeting you here." With that she put her hands on my face and gave me a warm kiss. My face turned red. I didn't know what to say or do, so I just held on to her.

"I was hoping I would see you here, Marie, but I didn't think it was going to happen. I wasn't sure I'd ever see you again."

"You haven't seen the last of me, my boy. I am not so easy to get rid of. I'm spending the night here, and heading back to Bozeman in the morning."

"I'm sorry, but it's was getting late, and my ride is leaving at 11:00."

"I have that suite again. Can't you skip the ride and stay with me?" I felt paralyzed. Spending another night with her was something that I had dreamt about since that magical night, but I did have an obligation to the CCCs.

When she saw me hesitating, she told me she would be making plans for the two of us to go to California one weekend. We agreed we would write to each other and try to figure that out. She walked me over to the truck. I hugged her tight and kissed her. There was something special about her, and I wished we could have spent another night together. Jack, already in the driver's seat, blasted the horn, and we were off. The wind was blowing hard on the three-hour ride back, and I nearly froze.

Rule 15
Respect Authority

June 24, 1933

Dear Larry,

I have been thinking about you and I hope you are feeling better. Hopefully the doctors find a cure for tuberculosis soon, so you will be good by the time I come home.

Yellowstone is an amazing and huge place. There are so many natural things here, including geysers, hot springs, mud pots, and something they call fumaroles, that stinking sulfur gas spews out of. The geysers are really incredible. They are filled with steam and water, and when they reach the surface, they erupt in a huge burst and the noise they make is deafening. Old Faithful is the most famous one. I couldn't believe it until I saw it myself. It erupts every 91 minutes or so, shooting water up to 185 feet into the air, and can last for up to 5 minutes.

I've also seen lots of wildlife, including herds of these huge bison. They kind of look like buffaloes, but the park ranger told us that they were a different species. They make a loud, strange noise when

they are looking for a mate, which is something that we men do not
have to do when looking for a woman. Then there are elk, which
look a lot like reindeer and make a sound which the rangers call
bugling. We've also seen wolves and coyotes, but they don't come too
close to people. There are two types of bears, the brown bear and the
grizzly bear. We've been told that they are dangerous, so we don't
feed them.

Yellowstone is a place that everyone should experience at least once in
their lifetime. So, here's my pledge to you. When I come home and
get a good job and when you feel stronger, I will take you and
Sammy here to see what I've been writing about. I want you to see
the snow-capped mountains and the lakes and the rivers and the
canyons. I want you to see it all. Keep this in mind and get better
soon.

Mike

Our life in the camp was far from easy. The work was hard,
the days were long, and the living conditions were primi-
tive. But, for the most part, our guys were able to deal with all
that. Then there was Sergeant Rosasco. He wasn't so easy to deal
with.

As I mentioned when I met him on Day 1, he was a short,
nasty son of a bitch. He was cruel, had a short temper, cursed all
the time, and treated us like we were in the army. He called us
"babies" or "little boys" so he could belittle us. Even though he
was Italian, he didn't treat us Italian guys any different than he
treated everyone else. He carried that damn wooden club with
him at all times, which he used to strike a few guys who dared to
disobey his orders or question his authority. He called his club
"Old Betsy," and told us it had taken him two weeks to carve it. It
even had notches on it, but we never figured out what they meant.

We hated that club and we hated him. I told the guys what he told me on the first day about his war experience, but that didn't change how we felt about him.

The way he wielded that club reminded me of *The Call of the Wild*, a book I read in 8th grade. It was told from the point of view of a dog named Buck who lived a happy life on a farm until he was kidnapped and sold to dog traders. They taught him to obey by beating him with a club. I don't remember the exact quote that Miss Reed discussed, but it was something like, "A man with a club is a lawmaker, a man to be obeyed, but not necessarily liked." I think she compared it to some countries, especially since it was soon after World War I had happened. But Rosasco was wrong in thinking that he could control us.

"That short little shit has a serious Napolean Complex," said Mario. "He tries to act so tough all the time to make up for his short height. He probably has a small dick too." That gave us all a good laugh and some of us would just whisper "Napolean" when he walked by. A few times he heard us and gave us a dirty look.

Then, Nicky Santora had a plan. The only time Rosasco was without his club was occasionally on a Sunday when he went to Mass. Of course, the fact that this awful guy would be religious struck us all as ironic. Anyway, Santora managed to get into his quarters and steal the club. A few of us followed him as he threw it into the river and cheered when it hit the water. Needless to say, Rosasco went nuts when he realized what happened.

"Who's the lowdown son of a bitch who did this?" he yelled when he got back to his quarters. "I will inspect everyone's goddamn bunk until I discover who's the goddamned culprit." He continued cursing and sputtering all kinds of stuff, and headed to our quarters to begin his search. The group of us who were witnessing his tirade desperately tried to not laugh, but it wasn't easy. When Ralphie couldn't hold it in, Rosasco gave him a dirty look and said, "You think this is funny?" With that we all broke down and laughed our asses off.

"I don't think he'll find that damn club," said Nicky, "unless he swims down the river."

We all laughed as he cursed and yelled. But it didn't last long, as the next day, we saw him headed off with his hatchet to get himself a new one. After a few days, his new club appeared. A man with a club is a law-maker, a man to be obeyed, but not necessarily liked

Rosasco was also drinking a lot. Sometimes he stumbled and sometimes he slurred his words. Nicky said he found a bottle of whiskey in his quarters when he went to steal his club. The other sergeants at the camp tried to avoid Rosasco whenever possible. He sat alone in the mess hall, while the others ate together. I could almost feel sorry for him, but not for long.

We had no choice but to deal with him on a daily basis. Some of us were terrified of him, and we knew we needed to keep our heads down and stay out of trouble if we wanted to survive. All in all, he was dangerous. I finally decided that a few of us should go see Captain Collins.

"Come in and welcome, Mike," he said. His office was decorated with fancy ribbons and certificates from his time in the service, along with photos on his desk probably of his wife and two young boys. We never thought of him as a family man until then, but it made sense. "Please remind me of your friends' names." Nick and Jimmy introduced themselves.

"What can I do for you? How are Yellowstone and the CCCs treating you?"

We were all a little bit nervous, but I was the first to speak "Sir, we've come to talk about Sergeant Rosasco. He has been rough on all of us, and we can see that the other sarges don't act that way."

"I see that he carries that club, but that's just for show, right? He likes to act tough. But I think he's all a bluff. Tell me more."

"No, he actually hits guys if they disobey him, and he's nasty."

"Really? I am sorry, but I had no idea." He rose from his chair and was silent.

Nick, Jimmy, and I told him about a few specific incidents, and he rubbed his chin probably thinking of what to do. "I promise I will keep a close eye on him to see what he does, and I will have a talk with him." Collins seemed like a decent guy, so we left feeling hopeful that something would be done about Rosasco.

The next day, a recruit named Giacomo arrived from the Bronx. He looked tough and strong and was a bit older than most of us. There was a rumor that he had been in a gang back home. Rosasco took an immediate dislike to him, probably because he sensed that Jake, the nickname he went by, was not the kind of kid who would submit to Rosasco's "Law of the Club." He made fun of Jake as often as he could by saying "I Gotcha Giacomo" in a sing-song voice, every time he caught Jake doing something he didn't like.

But Jake was not the kind of kid to take such treatment lying down. Finally, when Rosasco criticized him for the third time about his bunk not being perfect and mocked his name again, Jake stood up to him.

"Fuck you, you goddamn shithead. Who do you think you are? You're a washed-up old man, and everyone hates you."

With that, Rosasco went wild. He cold-cocked Jake right in the face, knocking him down, and then lifted the club high. I tried to grab the club, and he started throwing punches at me and a few of the other guys who were trying to disarm him. Jake joined in, put him down on the ground, and held him there. When Collins and some of the sarges arrived, they grabbed Rosasco and took him away while he was still cursing and struggling to get free.

This incident sent shockwaves through the camp. That's all anyone could talk about.

When we woke up the next morning, Rosasco was gone. Then we met his replacement, Sergeant John O'Brien, a nice guy from Washington State. Our nightmare was over, but that wasn't the end of the story for Rosasco.

Rather than kicking him out of the CCCs, they merely transferred him to Company 1506 at Bacon Rind Creek. About a week later, we heard rumors about the death of Abraham Yancovitch, an 18-year-old kid from Queens.

He was in a small remote CCC unit called a spike camp, so they were eating outside all the time. The way we heard the story, after breakfast on July 13, Yancovitch went to a nearby stream to wash his mess kit. The guys usually washed their mess kits below a small dam on the creek, but this time Yancovitch decided to clean his kit in the upper part of the creek which was closer. When Rosasco saw what Yancovitch was doing, he told him to stop. Yancovitch refused and said something nasty to Rosasco. An argument ensued and they took their fight into the woods where no one could see them. According to Rosasco, he punched Yancovitch in the right temple and knocked him out. Yancovitch was unconscious for a while, then somehow got back to his bunk. A few hours later, his friends found Yancovitch dead. The "official" report said he died of a fractured skull and a cerebral hemorrhage from a right-handed blow to the right temple.

But we all knew better.

"Oh sure," said Jimmy when we heard what happened. "Dying from a punch to the head? Knowing that bastard Rosasco, I'm sure he clubbed him to death."

"Since there were no witnesses, only Yancovitch knows what happened and he's dead," I said. "I heard that the government is doing an investigation, and they have already shit-canned Rosasco. His reign of terror is over."

A week later, I met a guy named Herb at the Fishing Bridge who filled me in with more details. "The Jewish boys in the camp held a vigil over Yancovitch's body on the night of his death. Singer and Bressler, two of Yancovitch's friends tried to rouse up the others to lynch Rosasco."

"Oh my God. What happened?"

"They found out that he was being held in the jail in Mammoth Hot Springs. When they got there, they were met by a local police force and were arrested and discharged. FBI agents who investigated them claimed that they were Communists."

"So, what happened to Rosasco?"

"The irony of this whole mess was that nothing happened to him, except that he agreed to resign. They issued a report saying that Yancovitch was disobedient and deliberately refused a lawful order. So, they blamed the victim."

Y ou see, sons, this wasn't the last time I saw this kind of injustice done. I know you boys heard me talk about some of the ways those in charge protect their own, and in the case of that no-good sergeant, literally get away with murder. I suspect the fact that Abraham Yancovitch as well as his defenders were Jews didn't help get any sympathy from the big shots. We all had heard anti-Semitic comments from many of them. I didn't mention it, but even our railroad cars heading out were segregated, with the black enrollees riding in the back car. It's a lousy world out there, and you'll all witness similar incidents in your lifetime. I've tried to bring you three up caring about all people and from what I've observed, you three have followed my example. Don't ever change.

We used to go fishing and have fish on a Saturday night. Then some of the boys played guitar and mandolin and we'd sing for hours. I started to like this life very much. When we went to bed at night, the boys all started to sing and crack jokes and we'd never fall asleep.

W e had gotten friendly with Victor, one of the chefs. He was Sicilian but was born in Argentina. He came to America just before the Depression and had worked at a fancy restaurant in San Francisco. One day he told the three of us he would fry up any fish we caught, as long as we didn't let anyone know about it. To us, this was a challenge. On the next weekend, we headed to the Fishing Bridge and tried our luck with just a few makeshift nets. The river was so clean and beautiful and peaceful. The closest thing we had back home was the Gowanus Creek, which was pretty disgusting.

Jimmy didn't hesitate, climbing onto a large boulder and tossing his net. "I see one and I think I got him," he said. "Now watch how an expert lands the big one." The next thing we knew, he slipped off the rock and went head-first into the river. Mario and I couldn't stop laughing, but Jimmy said, "I wanted to do that."

We each tried several times without success and were getting frustrated, when an old man named Bob, who looked like an Indian, offered some help. He had to be about 80 years old, with a scruffy white beard and wrinkled hands. "Let me tell you boys how to tickle a trout," he said. "Trout tickling is the easiest way to catch one, if you know the secret." We each tried to hold back a laugh.

But we were curious and at that point were willing to try anything. He squatted down and lay on his belly at the edge of a calm part of the river. Then he placed his hands on the bottom of the riverbed and waited.

"Now watch carefully," he whispered. "When a fish comes over my hands, I'll slowly rub its belly with the tips of my fingers." We huddled near him and watched his every move. "This puts the trout in a trance-like state, or what I call, a daydream." It wasn't long before we all saw a 12-incher approach his hand. He began tickling it for about 30 seconds. "Now I slowly hold him with both hands and take him right out of the water. Like this." He held the fish up high to show his catch and dropped it into his bucket. We were amazed. "Now it's your turn," Bob said, pointing to me.

I tried it, and after several lost fish and lots of coaching from Bob, I actually had one that I could try to rub.

"I think this guy is the one," I whispered, just as that one scuttled away. It took a lot of patience, but eventually, the rubbing worked and I had a 10-inch trout in my bare hands. I held it up high for the guys and added it to a bag. The whole experience was surreal. Here I was, a city kid in a distant land, using only my bare hands to mesmerize and catch a live fish. These trout were greenish-gray with a red slash along the jaw and dark spots along top and tail. They sort of looked like Rainbow Trout. The river was so plentiful that both Mario and Jimmy took their turns, and in about an hour, we had enough trout for Victor to cook for us.

After skinning and gutting our catch, he coated each in seasoned flour, eggs, and breadcrumbs. He pan-fried each filet with lots of lemons and capers. He served them with some sauteed squash and baked potatoes and a great bottle of white California wine. It was unforgettable and Victor became our best friend. We promised to keep our dinner to ourselves.

June 1933

One Sunday we went on a tour of the Park to see the scenery. We started by truck. First we visited The Dragon's Mouth Volcano. Then we stopped off at Sulfur Springs. Then we visited the Grand Canyon from the Upper and Lower Falls. Then we went to Artist Point and then Inspiration Point. Every place was prettier than ever. Then we stopped at a museum and saw many exhibits of stones, birds, and animals. Then we stopped at the Lower Geyser basin which had about 50 small geysers of all sorts and shapes. Then we passed some clear water pools as Morning Glory and Handkerchief Pool. Then we saw the Upper Geyser Basin which was prettier than the lower basin and many more things.

After, we visited a place called the Paint Pot which is a large pool of lava always bubbling up and has all colors.

Finally, we were off to "Old Faithful." At the place, there was a large Hotel and General Store, and a large Gas Station. And I got my first glimpse of Old Faithful. There were benches around the geyser about 100 feet away and people were waiting for the geyser to go off. During that time, we took a ride on some horses for hire and took pictures. I met some people from California, and talked to them for a while.

A bus arrived with a party of people from Hawaii. The girls were very pretty. I got to talking to them and they consented to take some pictures with me, and we had some sport. The boys were kidding me plenty. Finally, someone said the Geyser was going to go off. Everybody was watching eagerly. It was the prettiest thing I had ever seen. It shot away up in the air for over a minute then it ceased.

The people started to go, and we stood for a while and took more pictures with the Hawaiians and then we left. But we were told they were coming near our camp that evening. On our way back we stopped at some other waterfalls which were very nice. We saw some bears on the road and chased some. We arrived at camp hungry and tired.

That night we went to Fishing Bridge where they had the campfires and we saw the Hawaiian Girls again. They played music for us and sang. Then we took a walk with some of the girls and had a nice time. Got back to camp late. I got a package from Mom and she sent plenty of stuff including spaghetti and macaroni and salami and biscuits.

R eading my journal 30 years after I wrote it, I think this entry speaks for itself and needs little explanation. Simply stated, Yellowstone is magical! Old Faithful's boiling water shoots 90 to 100 feet into the air and it can discharge as much as 8,000 gallons of water at a time. Words cannot really capture it, and photographs are inadequate. I say we four agree to go to Yellowstone next year before the world becomes too much with us, whether with marriages and careers and children. This is a promise.

However, the Hawaiian girls are worth writing about. We were in the middle of the Depression. Hawaii was over 3,000 miles away, and of course, it wouldn't become a state until 1959. As big as the park is, it is really in the middle of nowhere. And yet, here they were. And were they ever beautiful! We were all stunned when we saw them getting off the bus, and a bunch of us headed right over to meet them.

"Aloha and welcome to Yellowstone, you lovely girls," Jimmy said. "My name is Jimmy. My associates, Mario, Duke, and I are residing in the park, so we will be your guides while you are visiting."

Of course, the girls laughed, as it was clear from our age and CCC uniforms that we were just kidding. We struck up a nice conversation with three of them, and they told us they had all just graduated from the Punahou School and were on this tour of the United States before they left for college. They told us their names were Abigail, Elizabeth, and Lydia. Lydia and I hit it off. They were all pretty, but Lydia was a real knockout. We invited them to meet us at the campfire that the Rangers had that night.

There was a crowd of over fifty CCC guys at the campfire that night, and sure enough, the girls came wearing grass hula skirts. At our urging, they walked to the front of the crowd and sang "My Little Grass Shack in Kealakekua Hawai'i" while performing a hula dance. The boys went wild! Mario, Jimmy, and I were the envy of everyone when the girls sat with us when they finished.

We had a great time, and after about an hour of telling stories and laughing, Lydia and I wandered off to be alone and had some fun. "Your *maka uliuli* are lovely," she said as she ran her fingers over my eyes.

"What does that mean?"

"It means I love your blue eyes, Duke. They look so fine in the moonlight." I was speechless, but I stroked her face and held her close to me. Her kisses were like none I've ever felt. She was beautiful in an exotic way with tan skin and long dark hair. I wanted to see her again.

"Lydia, can we meet here again tomorrow night?"

"I'm so sorry. This our last night in Yellowstone. Our bus leaves in the morning."

When they were going back to their hotel, Abigail took me aside.

"You do know that Lydia is a princess, Duke. She is a descendent of Princess Lili'uokalani, and is a very important person back home. She really loved being with you." With that, Lydia gave me a quick kiss, whispered "*a hui hou,*" and got on the bus. It wasn't until a few days later I learned her words meant "until we meet again."

Imagine! I was in Yellowstone Park and had been kissing a princess.

I had completely forgotten about Brooklyn and everything and everyone connected to it. The Brooklyn Rule about returning home was far from my mind. I thought about Mrs. Reed telling me I have *wanderlust* and added Hawaii to my list of places I would travel to someday, along with Rome, Sicily, Paris, and Cuba.

When I got back to camp, I was brought back to Brooklyn when I got a package of Italian food from Mama. It included a tin of biscotti, a link of pepperoni, a piece of soppressata, a chunk of provolone, some spaghetti, and a few cans of sauce.

The next day was Sunday so me and the boys shared the macaroni and tomato cans with Victor and asked him to make "Sunday Sauce" for the four of us. We stayed around and watched him make meatballs with ground beef, pork, and veal from his refrigerator along with breadcrumbs, eggs, and seasoning. He fried the meat in a bit of olive oil. The smell was incredible. Then, in a separate pan, he sauteed several garlic cloves and onions and then, the canned tomatoes along with some fresh basil, oregano, salt, and pepper. He put all the meat into the sauce and told us to come back in a few hours. For a little time on Sunday, I was back in Brooklyn, smelling Mama's sauce or what we called *gravy*. He used the two boxes of LaRosa spaghetti, and we brought a few friends to help us enjoy this feast. "This is perfect," I said. "The only thing missing is some great vino."

"Oh, I almost forgot," Victor said. A minute later he joined us at the table with two-gallon jugs of Gallo wine. "This is a new vintage from California. I know the CCCs are supposed to be alcohol-free zones, but I won't tell anyone if you guys don't." We all filled our glasses and had a wonderful time. We were stuffed by the time we finished.

Rule 16
Follow Your Religion

July 2-4, 1933

On Saturday July 1, we got our monthly pay, with the amount that was being sent home deducted. Everybody was in high spirits. On Sunday, we all went to Livingston. The town was celebrating their 50th Anniversary. The town was in an uproar. They started off with a big Parade which consisted of all the cowboys and cowgirls in the nearby towns and their children, all on horseback from age two and up. It was a treat to see kids riding horseback. Then a mob of Indians from a nearby reservation came down on old stage coaches and the young Indians were on horseback.

Then as usual there were some clowns or comedians in the Parade. Later we went to a restaurant and had a meal. Then we went to B Street and saw some girls we knew. We stayed there for a few hours, then we went to the Rodeo with the girls. The fun and thrills I saw in Rodeos in movies were not like this. It started by some of the Cowboys and Cowgirls giving some bareback riding, which was better than the circus riders. Then there was some bronco busting. Some of the cowboys were hurt very bad, busted heads and legs or ribs. Then there was steer roping and calf roping. Then steer dogging, then some relay racing on horseback. Meanwhile the clowns were always clowning. One of the clowns had his son there. His name was Little Hank, Jr. He was the child wonder of the West. He also played in moving pictures. I got the biggest kick out of the kid, more than anything else in the Rodeo. Later I got a picture of the kid and he autographed it. Then the Indians came out and started going crazy, riding full speed and war dances and making all kinds of noises. Later, after some more races, the Rodeo was over. It was the best and the first one I ever seen.

We went to a hotel for the night, then we had supper. Then we went out and took the town over by storm. We went to a dance. It was swell, but too crowded for dancing, but very sociable. I walked one girl to her ranch which was 2 miles away. On the way home, we stopped at the lakeside park. We had a nice time then finally we left for her home. I got back to the hotel at 3:30. The boys kidded me along as usual, But I didn't mind. It was worth it.

Next day we saw another parade; walked around town. Some of the boys got into an argument and cut some guys up and we got marked lousy by the town Police. At 6 p.m. we left Livingston to go back to camp. After 5 hrs. of mountain tiding and cold breeze, we arrived at camp.

When I decided to join the CCCs, I felt like it would be strict, like being in basic training in the army. We'd be restricted to the base, we'd have limited leave, and there definitely would be no girls. After one month had passed, all of those misgivings were gone. We had lots and lots of free time and we were free to go wherever we wanted to go. If we took a day off, they just docked us for a day's pay, and clearly, there were girls everywhere, and they were all over us New York guys. I've already mentioned Marie, Sandy, and Jane, and then there was Lydia,

Abigail, Elizabeth, and Carol. Many of us took three-day week-ends and went off with the girls. Jimmy seemed to have a different girl every weekend.

On the other hand, Mario and Sandy were inseparable, and Mario was head over heels in love with her. We made fun of him for his "one-girl policy" but he didn't care. He said he had finally found the one, and he wasn't going to let anyone or anything come between them. The truth was that unlike me and Jimmy, he didn't go out with any girls back home, so she was his first.

Sandy was a real beauty with hazel eyes and long flowing, blond hair, not like any of the Italian girls we knew back home. Her eyes sparkled, she had a great smile and turned heads wherever she went. Plus, she was a total sweetheart, kind and compassionate, and always putting others before herself. She had a way of making everyone around her feel special. Mario was a lucky guy to have her in his life. She became his best friend, his confidante, and his lover. She made him laugh, she made him cry, and she made him feel like the luckiest man in the world. He knew that he could always count on her, and he was so grateful to have her in his life. In a way, I was jealous that I had yet to find someone like her. I wondered if I ever would. Might Marie be the one? I was no longer thinking about Pauline in that way.

Each work day began with reveille at 6:00, followed by assembly at 6:15 where we would get that day's work assignments. Breakfast followed at 6:30, and we were off to work at 7:00. I was made foreman of a work gang which was not so easy, but I got along with the boys alright. Our work assignments were always a surprise. We might be planting seedlings or building flood barriers or digging out rocks for a roadway or clearing dead wood or removing or spraying brush for new paths. Whatever the job was, we mostly groaned. We worked brutally each day.

For example. planting seedlings sounded easy enough, but it

proved back-breaking. I estimated that I could plant 50-60 of these tiny sticks in an hour for a total between 400-500 each day. If there were 20 of us on a typical day, you can do the math. "I want to go on record that they should name this forest The James Cala Forest," said Jimmy, after a long, hot day. "My sweat helped irrigate these little bastards and when they grow up, I want to be remembered."

Then there were those forest fires that could pop up at any time, from a lightning bolt or through the negligence of some dumb camper. We were spared for the first few weeks, but on some days, we practiced how to stop a fire. We were always ready. Each of us was given a tool called a Pulaski to practice. It was invented by some guy named Ed Pulaski during what was called "The Big Burn" in 1910. That fire burned three million acres in North Idaho and Western Montana, and in just 36 hours, it killed at least 78 men. We practiced using it, but it wasn't easy. The hoe part goes into the ground to make the fire line. It scrapes away anything that could burn off the surface, and the ax chopped away little trees, roots, and shrubs. I hoped I'd never have to use one in a real fire.

On Friday, July 14, the priest came to camp and we received Holy Communion which made me feel pretty good for the day. That night I received mail from friends and Marie G. Her letter was pretty sad and made me feel bad about it.

Things went along pretty nicely for the next 4 or 5 days. I received Holy Communion the following week also.

Having been raised a Catholic, I had to get up the nerve to go to Confession before I received Communion. Given my sexual adventures during the past month, I had to make a decision. Do I tell some priest about what I had done? Or do I skip Mass altogether? Back in Brooklyn, confessing was easy. I knew old Father Hart didn't ask any follow-up questions like, "What exactly did you do with that girl that constituted "impure actions?" or "How many times did you have those impure thoughts?" Or, "Who were you thinking impure thoughts about?" He was famous for giving easy penance, like "five *Our Fathers* and five *Hail Marys.*" But this priest was not Father Hart, so I had to go to the tent he was in and tell all. When I entered the tent, I was taken aback because there was no curtain or sliding window to keep us from seeing each other.

"Come sit with me, young lad, and let's talk about what is on your mind," the priest said in a kind voice with an Irish accent. "I am John O'Malley." He was maybe 30 and not like any of the old priests at St. Fortunata who were all distant and self-righteous.

I began with the usual, "Bless me, Father."

But he interrupted me and said, "Son, let's just talk about what's on your mind."

I was shocked. I didn't know what to say or do. I thought about saying something like, "Sorry," and walking out of the tent, but he seemed so kind and, I didn't want to offend him and probably add another sin to my current litany of misdeeds. I took a deep breath and began to talk about my night with Marie, the heavy petting with several other girls, and of course, all those lustful thoughts.

Then he said, "Son, all of these sins deal with sex, which is a natural instinct that young men have. It's normal. But you said nothing about the rest of the Commandments. What about honoring your parents or making false statements, or killing or stealing? Those are the big ones." My immediate thought was about the Brooklyn Rules. Would not going home to my parents be considered sinfull?

"I'm sorry, Father, can you say that again?"

He chuckled. "Somehow, you and most young men your age focus on the evils of sex, and that's the one trait that Almighty God gave us. Sex before marriage is a recent taboo, but many religious folks only teach about that one."

My main exposure to religious education was in preparation for Communion and Confirmation, and yes, those nuns spent so much time warning us about the evils of sex, so much that even thinking what they called "impure thoughts" were just as bad as "impure actions." Now this priest was telling me something quite different.

We continued my confession, which was really a friendly conversation now. He gave me some advice about not emotionally hurting any women. He told me that he was proud of the work I was doing in the CCCs, and said he'd be happy to talk whenever I had any issues.

"Aren't you supposed to give me some penance," I asked as we were finishing up. "We can skip it this time." And that's what we did, and I felt relieved when it was over, especially because we soon had to face our first forest fire. Whenever Father O'Malley came to the camp, I made sure to have a chat with him. I felt he was more than just a priest. He was the big brother I never had.

Rule 17
Save Time For Fun

I must tell you boys again, that most days and nights in Yellowstone were tough Sometimes, we'd wake up in the morning or be awoken in the middle of the night to contain raging fires, and we'd probably spend several nights there sleeping under the stars, hungry and freezing. Or we might be climbing up and trimming diseased trees, or digging and clearing a wooded area to make a road, or planting thousands of seedlings in a burnt-out area. None of this was fun. I was getting stronger each day, which was a good thing. There's a Latin phrase, *mens sana in corpore sano* meaning a healthy mind in a healthy body. I gained so much physically and emotionally during my time there. Looking back, I had been forming my future with that hard work.

But for many of the boys, enough to convince them to quit and go home. I remember a conversation I had with James Gatto, a guy from somewhere in Connecticut, who everybody liked. He had brought along a mandolin and played it whenever he could. We all enjoyed it, whether late at night in the bunkroom or around a campfire. We would sing along to old songs and even some Italian ones. He was so talented, and made me wish I had some musical skills.

After dinner one night, I saw him crying in his bunk. "Are

you all right, Gatz?–What's the matter? Is someone back home really sick or something?"

"No, Duke. I just don't think I can take the CCCs anymore. This work is too hard for me. Every bone in my body hurts. I miss my girlfriend, Madeline, and I think I am going home tomorrow."

"Wait a minute. We need to talk. You are so important here in building up everyone's morale. I can't imagine this place without you and your mandolin and your singing. You've already come this far, so it would be ashamed to leave now. And what will you do for work if you leave?"

"My dad has a small music store, and I can help him out and maybe give lessons. Madeline really loves me. We keep writing to each other as often as we can. We hoped we would get married when I got home. But I can't wait until September."

I did my best to persuade him to stay, but I failed. He was gone the next morning before any of us could say goodbye. And we did miss him a lot.

He wasn't alone in leaving. We lost many guys at that point, many because they heard of higher-paying jobs back home, many because they couldn't take the hard work, and many simply because they were homesick. On a few bad days, I even considered leaving.

But, those of us who stayed understood we were doing important work, and the money home was helping our families. And we tried to get the most of what the camp offered. As I looked over my journal, I realized I left many of those day-to-day details out, probably because I was exhausted when I hit my bunk, and mostly because I wanted to remember weekends and trips into the local towns. So, the details from June to September were sketchy about the work. I don't recall why I omitted some of the great activities the camp provided.

Once the Recreation Building was finished in mid-June, we suddenly had lots to do on the down-time we had. When you walked in the door, there was a Canteen that sold candy, cigarettes, combs, and other items. There was an area that had athletic equipment that we could borrow so we could play sports on the camp fields. We had a dozen baseballs, six bats, and ten gloves, so we broke into teams and have a game when we had time. Some of the boys were picked to play ball with some other camps. Soon they even got some makeshift uniforms. We also had access to boxing gloves, and we would set up a ring and watch some of us compete. There was always something to do at the camp, and whenever we got bored, we went for a swim in the river or the lake.

One section of the rec building was set up as a classroom, which offered a series of subjects focused on learning a skilled trade preparing us for returning home. So, guys were trained to be licensed electricians, plumbers, welders, or carpenters. They camp brought in union trainers and supplied the books and even gave those who completed the course a set of tools. Nicky Vitale, a buddy from my neighborhood, was learning to be a welder and told me that his uncle helped to build the Empire State Building, and had already signed him up for a job when he got his union card. Vinny Scotto was training to be an electrician and he would soon have his union card.

The camp leaders strongly encouraged those who could not read or write to take literacy classes, which met three nights a week. Initially, I was surprised that many boys were illiterate. Learning to read and write was a serious issue especially if they were going to be able to pursue some kind of career after leaving the CCCs. A few of my friends back in Brooklyn had dropped out of school when they were in the 4th or 5th grade, which sounds unbelievable now, but it was during the Depression, and if their parents spoke only Italian, they ended up doing the same. The CCCs brought in a group of professors from the university in Missoula to teach those classes. Each class had about a dozen students in it and there were actually two sections going on at the same time: one for beginners and one for advanced.

The camp also offered academic courses including English composition, spelling, business arithmetic, trigonometry, Spanish and citizenship. I enrolled in the English Composition course taught by Professor Stephen Booth and learned so much about what to do and what not to do when writing. There were only a few of us in that class, so he gave us each special help. In looking over a story I handed in, Booth wrote "I have bad news for you, young man. You are destined to become a writer." I wasn't sure what he meant until years later when my job, my children, and life itself stood in my way to write. We read several short stories and Booth taught us about experiencing a work rather than analyzing its meaning. All these years later, I still use strategies I learned, many of which have helped me write this book. I even considered finishing school when I got home, but that never happened.

The new library near the main entrance was my favorite spot. I loved reading magazines and newspapers to see what was going on back in civilization. My favorite magazine was *Harper's*, but I also liked thumbing through *Collier's, Time, Newsweek,* and *The American Mercury*. We got some local Montana papers, as well as the *Chicago Tribune*. The *Tribune* was the best for national and sports news. I tried to keep up with the news of what was happening in the world, which wasn't always good. There were stories of gangsters Pretty Boy Floyd killing an FBI agent and three local policemen in Kansas City, and Machine Gun Kelly kidnapping an Oklahoma oilman and demanding a $200,000 ransom. In July, a guy named Wiley Post became the first person to fly solo around the world, landing at an airfield in my home town of Brooklyn. I loved seeing Brooklyn make history.

The good news in sports was that on June 8, the American Max

Baer scored a technical knockout over Germany's Max Schmeling, before a crowd of 56,000 at Yankee Stadium. But baseball was my favorite sport, especially covering my beloved Brooklyn Dodgers. I loved checking the scores and the standings. My boys weren't very good that year, but I still loved them. The papers were delivered by train several days a week, so they were always a few days late. But I didn't care. I loved reading about the world and my favorite teams.

I was surprised when I read the Thursday, July 7th *Trib* that there had been what was the first All-Star Game between the best players in the National league and the best in the American League. The game took place at Comiskey Park right near the Chicago World's Fair that we had been to. The *Tribune* called it the game of the century and said that it was designed to be to boost morale during the Depression. They said that they had to switch different baseballs because apparently the National League baseball is a different size than the American League baseball. They also had to switch umpires, so they had American League umpires and National League umpires and they would switch off behind home plate. The highlight of the game apparently was when Babe Ruth hit a two-run home run at the bottom of the third inning. Of course, it was Babe Ruth. The New York Yankees' Lefty Gomez was the winning pitcher, and my boy, Tony Cuccinello was the only player representing the Dodgers, but he went hitless.

A fter dinner most nights, the boys and I went to play some pool or ping-pong. Some of the boys spent free time lifting weights, which seemed crazy, given how much heavy lifting of logs and trees we had to do each day.

But the real treat was the Wednesday night movies, though it was far from Dish Night back in Brooklyn. The government had a deal with the Hollywood brass, so each week we would get first-run movies. Most of the guys took advantage of them, so we had a great time together.

We saw *Gold Diggers of 1933*, *Charlie Chan's Greatest Case*, Laurel and Hardy's *Sons of the Desert*, and many others that I have forgotten about. The biggest hit was *She Done Him Wrong*, starring my idol, Mae West. When they announced what the picture would be, even guys who never went to the movies showed up, and they had to get more chairs for us. The movie began with some Gay 90's music and then pictures of the cast. Of course, Mae's picture as Lady Lou was first, and the fellows hooted and yelled when they saw her. Then there were lots of funny scenes in the Bowery, and then lots of talk in a bar, much of it about how beautiful Mae was and then we saw a quick shot of a nude painting of her over the bar, When the piano guy started playing "After the Ball is Over," we caught a quick glance of Mae smoking and smiling, and we all went wild. But it was about ten minutes before we actually saw or heard her, and the boys were getting restless. When she made her entrance in a horse-drawn carriage, the place erupted. Practically every line she spoke had some sort of sexual meaning to it, and we laughed at them all. Lines like "Why don't you come up and see me some time?" and "You said I had a soul. I looked for it, but I didn't find it." One of my favorite scenes was near the end when Mae sang a sexy version of "Frankie and Johnny." After a series of assorted crimes going on, instead of going off the prison like the rest of her gang, the cop, played by a young Cary Grant, decides he wants her for himself, and they drive off together. We went crazy at the ending.

A few weeks later, we were treated to another Mae West picture, *I'm No Angel*, and then again, the place was mobbed. You see, we got to see girls on some weekends, but we still were a bunch of hard-working young men whose hormones were running wild. So, when Mae said, "When I'm good, I'm very good. But, when I'm bad, I'm better," or "It's not the men in your life that counts, it's the life in your men," we roared.

Another treat was in August when we saw *King Kong*. A few weeks before I left home, Grace, got free passes for Pauline and me to go to the brand-new Empire State Building 86th floor Observation Deck where she worked selling souvenirs. The view from the 86th floor was amazing, but it was even more amazing when we took another elevator to the 102nd floor observatory. The view from the 102nd floor was breathtaking, and we could see all five boroughs of New York City and even New Jersey. It was a bit scary to be so high up, but it was amazing.

Seeing Kong climbing that building was one of the best parts of the movie, but the scenes in the jungle were pretty good too. We all hooted when Kong lifted up Fay Wray's dress to take a peek. Years later when you boys and I saw it on television, they apparently cut that scene out. After we saw *King Kong*, we couldn't stop trying to figure out how they made it look so real.

One of the last movies we saw was called *Wild Boys of the Road*, and it was the saddest of them all. It was set in the present, and was all about what youngsters were doing during the Depression. The main character's mother had been out of work for months. And then his father lost his job. Then the young boy and his high school friends decided to hop the freight and look for work. Wherever they went, they met kids just like them.

It hit home because we had seen many "boxcar kids" like them on our ride west. We passed them on trains heading the opposite way, and we saw them huddled alongside the tracks as we passed many stations. After setting up camps for a while, the police would come and chase them away, so they jumped on other trains, not knowing or caring where they were headed. The movie was so realistic, and showed the terrible situation that the country was in. They camped at "Sewer City," a place where they could live in empty giant concrete sewer pipes. The movie had sort of a happy ending--the boys get arrested and a kind judge gets them jobs, but we all knew that we were the lucky ones. Thanks to the CCCs and the training we were getting, we might not end up like all those poor kids.

Rule 18
Be Part of a Team

Then one night we were called out to go and fight a forest fire.
Everybody was excited and everyone wanted to go, thinking it would
be easy. But we found out different. We got there about 6 o'clock.
The trucks couldn't go any further. We all got off and then the fun
began. The fire was on a peak of a mountain called Pelican Peak.
We started to climb hills and mountains which were very steep and
we had to tie ropes to the trees so that the boys could climb. Boys were
falling, one after another, exhausted from
climbing. The air was getting thinner the higher we went. Finally
about ten o'clock after four hours of climbing, we arrived at the fire.
We were very tired and hungry and thirsty.

We had some water, but we had to be careful with it because there
wasn't any up there in case we ran short. We were up 11,000 feet
above sea level. Thousands of trees were blazing and plenty of smoke.
It was some sight to see. We were put in squads and separated and
we were shown what to do. Some were put on ax crews, some pickax
crews, some on road work, and I was put on the powder crew
blasting rows of trees and rock. The noise was getting the best of me.
We were hungry as hell, the food didn't arrive yet. They were

sending it upon mules and pack horses also. We were getting one hour rest after working 6 hours then work again.

———

T he clanging alarm woke us up at 3:00 am.
"This is not a drill," yelled Sergeant O'Brien. "There's a big ass fire up near the Pelican Peak, and we need to hustle up and get here."

"Can we at least go to the head?" asked one of the guys.

"Yes, but make it quick. This is serious stuff."

We had been expecting to fight some fires, but this one came out of nowhere. I was so much stronger than when I first signed on, and we had done so much preparation and so many calisthenics, but I wasn't prepared mentally. I don't say this in my journal, but I was so scared, I even cried when I was out of sight of my team. I've never told this to anyone, but after the first day at the fire site, I even thought about heading back to camp and returning to Brooklyn.

All the hours of lectures, trainings, calisthenics, and practice sessions had led us to this day. Battling this horrific fire would be our first real test as CCC men. As much as we griped about the work up to this moment, we were about to enter something that put our lives in danger.

We quickly got dressed, grabbed our packs and tools, and headed for the trucks. The sarge directed us to get on in groups of ten. I could have driven in the cab, but I decided to stay with my team in the rear. It was pitch dark while we drove that rattling old truck for about 15 miles. Everyone in the back was quiet, though no one was sleeping. Some guys were silently praying, and a few guys were silently sobbing. I didn't think of myself as being religious, but that night I was happy I had received Communion on Sunday.

We had heard some thunder, so we figured it must have been started by lightning. We saw the light from the fire in the distance and as we got closer, we started to smell it, and then actually feel the heat. Everyone was tense.

"Where the Fuckowi?" Franky, the comic in our camp, started yelling, and we all laughed. It was a line from an old joke about a lost Indian tribe, and it briefly lightened the mood. Then the trucks suddenly stopped. They couldn't go any further, yet we were far from the fire. It was 6:00 and the sun was rising.

"This is it men." O'Brien said. "We got a long way up this mountain, so stay together and stay safe."

The trails up the mountain were overgrown, and the hike towards the blaze wasn't easy. A few guys would go ahead and tie ropes around the trees, so we could pull ourselves up the steeper areas. But still, some of the guys lost their footing and fell back down several yards. At that point, I heard Franky and his friend Albert talking about giving up. I didn't pay too much attention to them, but soon after, I noticed they were gone.

"Hey, Sarge," I said. "I didn't see them go, but Franky and Albert must have headed back."

"Well, screw them. We have an impossible job to do and I can't think about them," he said. "Let's keep climbing."

We found out later they walked all the way back to our camp, and then packed up and headed back to Brooklyn. As I said, there was no serious penalty for deserters except their $30 a month was stopped, they received a dishonorable discharge, and they had to pay their own way home. The official policy was if they returned within 10 days, they could get reinstated. The real damage those deserters caused was for the morale for those of us left behind. I was so pissed that these guys had abandoned us, just when we needed them.

Finally the food arrived the next afternoon. Some of the mules fell over the mountain with food and all so we couldn't get much to eat. We were getting tired but we had to keep on working and I mean work. Some of the boys deserted the fire, they went back to the camp they hiked all the way back a distance of 24 miles but we had to carry on. The Rangers were always on top of us hollering their brains out telling us the quicker we got it out, the quicker we went home. We prayed for rain but it never came.

As we got closer to the fire, the sounds got louder and louder, and the guys all got quieter and quieter. All we could hear was the crackling, sputtering, and snapping of the roaring blaze. Then, we felt a blast of intense heat and the overwhelming smell of burnt pine hitting right in our faces. We choked on the acrid smoke and had trouble breathing. Some of us tried to block out the smoke with our dirty handkerchiefs. My heart was beating like mad, partly by the fire and partly by the altitude. I had never been so scared in my life, and I know I wasn't alone. Jerry, a sweet kid from the Bronx, was actually crying. Mario had this frightened look on his face as he stared into space.

But we trudged on.

Then suddenly, huge flakes filled the sky and fell on our heads. Some of the open spaces had already turned white with the ashes.

"Holy shit! It's snowing," I said." "The guys around me laughed.

"Let's build a snowman," someone said.

"OK, cut the crap, you guys," sarge said, "and carry on. We have to move at least 100 yards closer to where a station has been set up."

With each step, the heat came through my boots. When we reached the fire station, the ranger in charge gave us our orders and told us to begin the fire line. We had learned how to make one in class, but now it was actually happening. A few of the guys carried hand-saws and two or three carried shovels. The rest of us each carried a Pulaski, that heavy tool with an ax blade and a hoe.

As twenty of us began scraping and chopping, the guys with the shovels followed and made a wide ditch. I was assigned to the powder crew which meant me and another guy had to use dynamite to blast large stumps and boulders in the ditches. It was exhausting work, especially with the noise, the heat, the smoke, and the fear of what we were doing wouldn't stop the fire. After about two hours, our line was done, and we just collapsed. We moved back about 50 yards from the ditch and waited. And waited. And waited.

While we were waiting, a team of horses carrying food arrived, and we chowed down on some buttered bread, hard-boiled eggs, coffee, and ice-cold orange juice. The sad part of all this was that earlier, three mules carrying food had fallen off the mountain. We felt bad for the mules but worse for ourselves because they lost our food. It was approaching evening and we hadn't eaten the entire day. But we had to eat quickly as there was much more to do.

The roar of the forest fire was deafening. This fire is totally out of control," said the ranger in charge of our small troop. He had been working since dawn he told us. "We have to clear the breaks if we are going to stop its progress. We need more help with dynamiting tree stumps and boulders."

"I'm ready to go," I said.

"That's good. I asked for help from the colored troop leader, the ranger said. "I want you to work with this guy," he said, pointing to a stocky, well-built Black man.

I was taken aback by this order of working with a Negro. I had seen the segregated colored troop on our train and a few days ago at the Fishing Bridge campfire, but I didn't imagine our troop would ever be working with those guys. I had heard the CCCs would be segregated, but seeing a large group of colored guys in CCC uniforms was kind of shocking. Later at the campfire, a lot of the Brooklyn guys said some nasty stuff about those colored guys. I don't even want to print what they were saying.

"OK, sir," I said with some hesitation. I didn't like this, but I couldn't say no. I kept wondering what my friends would be saying about me working with this colored man.

I turned to my new partner, who was looking like he wasn't happy about this arrangement either. "Pack this equipment here," I said. "We need to take about a dozen sticks of dynamite. And you have to be very careful with this stuff. Be sure you don't drop it."

"I've been working on demolition for the past three weeks," he said with a bit of a nasty tone in his voice. "I got this."

I suddenly felt awful. Here was this man who probably had the same training I had, and I was talking to him like he was 12-year-old Sammy.

I was raised in the East New York section of Brooklyn, a neighborhood nearly all Italian with some Irish nearby. My school was all white, as was St. Fortunata's, our local church. I only shopped in all-white stores. All my friends were white. I rarely spoke to Black people. I later learned my partner was born in Harlem, but his family had moved to the South Bronx when he was young. His experience was similar to mine, except it was totally Black.

As we grabbed all our tools and TNT and walked towards the fire break that was being dug, we kept apart from each other. The trek took about 20 minutes and neither one of us spoke. When we came to the first stump, we put down our tools and looked at each other, suspiciously.

"Hey man, I'm Mike LoMonico, but you can call me Duke," I said, extending my hand. "So, you've been doing this demolition already?" I felt like this guy wasn't happy to be working with me. He had been acting sullen all this time.

He hesitated for a moment, but then weakly shook my hand. "I'm John Scott," he said, "and everyone calls me Scotty. Yes, I was blowing shit up all day yesterday."

I smiled and said, "Well, let's get to it."

We worked for about an hour without saying much to each other. We'd find an old stump, use the axe to cut some deep notches into it, insert several sticks of dynamite, and with a slow fuse to get clear, we blasted it. After about two hours, we took a break and sat on a log. We broke out some sandwiches and started talking to each other.

"You know, Scotty, I was a bit worried about working with you at first."

"Why's that?"

"Well, I know Negros don't like white people," I said, sort of joking.

Scotty shook his head and smiled. "Yeah, I know white people don't like Negros either. And, by the way, I don't like being called "a Negro." If you want to describe me, just call me Black."

We stared at each other. The silence was broken when we heard the roar of a tree top bursting into flame. Almost simultaneously, we laughed.

"By the way," said John, "I didn't like the way you spoke to me back at the camp. You were totally patronizing."

"Oh, yeah, I'm sorry about that. I can sometimes be a bit of an asshole."

"Well, you sure were back there in front of all your white buddies."

Each time we took a break, we shared our experiences about growing up before and after the Great Depression began. It seemed both in the Bronx and in Brooklyn, the challenges we faced were not very different. Neither of us could find work, and we both had to endure bread lines. We joined the CCCs to get out of New York and get paid a dollar a day, with most of that money was being sent home to help our families.

We knew we needed each other to get this demolition job done, and we began to like each other. When the conversation came to families and schooling, I asked Scotty where he went to school. His answer was not one I expected.

"I was fortunate to attend Regis High School on East 84th Street," he said. "It's a wonderful school run by the Jesuits. All students are on scholarship there, so there's no tuition. I graduated in 1929, just before the Crash."

I didn't know what to say. He looked at me without saying anything, and finally I told him I only went up to 8th Grade at PS 34.

As the sun began to set and the fire began to die down, we headed back to the base camp where most of the guys were eating. We sat on a log, away from the rest of the troop, drinking water and eating sandwiches. He was still the only Black guy there and most of the White guys were staring at us.

"You know what? I'm glad we worked together today," I said loudly. "You're a good guy."

Scotty smiled. "Thanks. You're not so bad yourself."

As we finished our sandwiches, we felt a sense of camaraderie that hadn't been there before. We had worked together to fight a fire, and in the process, we had become friends. I noticed the dirty looks I was getting from my friends. I could even hear them mumbling nasty comments about this Negro (although, that's not the word they used) who "didn't belong here." As Scotty was getting ready to head back to his segregated camp, I gave him a hug and thanked him for his hard work. Everyone just stared at us.

We continued to see each other around Yellowstone. We found ourselves talking more and more, sharing stories and jokes, and learning more about each other's lives. We became close friends. We laughed and joked, and even shared our hopes and dreams for the future. He talked about his desire to become a lawyer, and I shared my ambition to be a writer.

When our time in Yellowstone came to an end, we exchanged phone numbers and promised to stay in touch. We even hoped we would be working together again in the future. Unfortunately, that never happened. To this day, I wonder what became of John Scott.

Finally after 3 days of hell and fire it started to rain and it fell like barrels at a time. That helped us a great deal. The fire was finally out and we started to go back to the camp hiking down the mountain again falling half asleep and dog tired. It started raining again, we got on the open trucks and were on our way to the camp soaked, half dead and almost asleep. We got some reception when we got back. After a hot shower and nice meal I went to bed and fell asleep like a log. The next day we took it easy.

Rule 19
Be Open to New Ideas

On a Thursday night, a few days later, we headed to a mandatory assembly after dinner. Of course, it was our free time, so we grumbled all the way to the main building. We got in our seats and Collins came and spoke.

"Evening, men," he began. "First of all, I want to commend you on the excellent work you did with the fire last week. As you know, a few of your colleagues couldn't hack it, and they decided to go home. But you who stayed worked tirelessly and deserve praise. It took a lot of guts to do what you men did. Therefore, I am giving you off tomorrow so you can have a three-day weekend."

The boys cheered and applauded, and we got up and started to head out.

"Wait," he said. "One more thing." More groans and hisses and laughs.

"I want to introduce you to someone from the US Forest Service, who will talk to you about another critical mission: insects."

We went wild and laughed again. When we settled down, he introduced us to this government guy who told us all about beetles. He had on wireless glasses and was wearing a three-piece suit that seemed out of place here.

"Hello, boys. I am Dr. Philip Santangelo. I am a scientist with the United States Forest Service, here today to talk to you about pine beetles."

"Pine beetles?" shouted Ronny Gallo, "What the hell are they?" This poor guy ignored the comment and stayed cool.

"These are small insects that can cause a lot of damage to trees and forests. They are attracted to stressed or weakened trees, and once they find a suitable host, they bore into the bark and lay their eggs."

We were getting restless. Everyone was ready for that three-day weekend and wanted nothing to do with this guy or his bugs. We had recovered from those days stopping the fire and wanted to celebrate.

"So why is that a problem?" someone shouted. Someone else yelled, "Why should we give a shit?"

Collins stood up and warned us to be respectful. Then he took over asking questions before the hooligans shouted them out. "Sorry for that outburst, doctor. Please tell us why this is so important?"

"Here in Yellowstone Park, we have a serious bark beetle infestation. It is a small insect that bores into the bark of trees, killing them."

"How can they destroy a whole forest?" the captain asked.

"These buggers are efficient at killing trees. They can kill a single tree in a matter of weeks or months. Once a tree dies, it becomes a breeding ground for other insects and diseases. This can lead to a chain reaction that can destroy an entire forest."

"So, what can our boys do to rid these little bastards?"

"Thanks for that question, Captain Collins. One way is to plant resistant species of trees. That's part of our plan and our job. But your job in Yellowstone is to remove dead or dying trees and burn them."

He had a few more scientific things to say that nobody understood, and then Collins thanked him and took over.

"This work is dangerous and difficult," he said. "You will have to climb high into trees to reach the infected areas and deal with the poison these beetles produce. The poison can cause skin rashes, respiratory problems, and even death. Thank you, men, for listening." There was some polite applause, mostly because he was done.

"That's all for now, men. Enjoy your three-day weekend and we'll give you some instructions next week. Dismissed."

Our beetle hunting would begin on Monday and continue for the next two weeks. It wasn't easy work, and it was dangerous. We didn't see it, but we heard a CCC man named Marty Yaro in another camp died when a tree that was being cut fell on him, and another kid fell out of a tree and broke his leg. These beetles led to danger.

Captain Collins had told us to look forward to danger, poison, and death and then said, "Have a fun weekend, boys." Really? But in spite of what he had told us, we did have a good time. Actually, I had an amazing time. And I learned something important about myself, as a writer.

Me, Jimmy, Mario, and a few other boys took a bus to the West Gate of Yellowstone and headed to Jackson Hole, Wyoming. The bus ride was long and hot and bumpy, but we didn't mind. We were too excited about our upcoming adventure. We talked and laughed the whole way, and by the time we arrived in Jackson Hole, we were all feeling pretty good.

The first thing we did was find the nearest bar. After a few beers, we asked the bartender for some suggestions for us to go. He told us we'd have a good time at the Bar B-C Dude Ranch and showed us where we could get a ride that would get us there. We had a great three days at the ranch, and in some ways, it changed my life. We got back to camp around midnight on Sunday knowing that we would be up early the next morning.

———

This trip changed my life. Something magical happened that weekend, and even though it took me over 30 years, one kind person gave me the courage to write this book. I met a woman, who along with her husband, opened me up to a whole new world. That's a long story and I will tell you what happened. But first I'll tell you how it began.

When we got off the bus, Jimmy, Mario, and I said goodbye to the other CCC guys we traveled with and headed right to the Million Dollar Cowboy Bar. I never found out why it was called "Million Dollar," but maybe because it looked like a million dollars inside. It had this long wooden bar with all these carved cowboy images on it—horses and bison and pistols and lariats. Hanging above the bar was a line of elk antlers, as far as I could see. The floor was covered in peanut shells. There were slot machines off to the right of the bar and lots of gambling tables as well, with men and women playing poker and other card games.

The bartender was exactly what you would imagine in a cowboy bar. His name was Hank, and he had a really long mustache and wore a black Stetson hat. We asked him for three beers and he said, "Do you want to try some of what we call "Moose Drool?"

We all laughed and Jimmy asked, "How do they get close enough to the moose to catch the drool?" Hank immediately had a good comeback, probably a line he had been using for years.

"We don't actually use real moose drool," he said with all seriousness. "We just add some moose shit to the bottom of the barrel to give it some character. We found it was so much easier to harvest the moose shit. People around here just love it, but if we called it 'Moose Shit Beer,' they might not."

Jimmy and I each ordered a glass, but we had to convince Mario that Hank was putting us on. So, we ordered three Moose Drools, and they weren't too bad. When Hank asked us what we were doing in Jackson Hole, we told him we were working at the CCC camp in Yellowstone. He was impressed. "This next round is on me," he said. "You boys must be working hard each day, and our country is proud of you."

"Thanks, Hank," I said. "We came all the way from Brooklyn, so everything we have been seeing is new to us. We have a 3-day weekend, so we thought we'd come here. Any suggestions of things we should see around these parts?"

"Have you boys ever been to a dude ranch? There's a great one not too far from here, and many of my out-of-town customers rave about it."

We three looked at each other and smiled. "Let's do it," Jimmy said.

"There's a horse-drawn wagon that leaves town every hour and will take you right to the Bar B-C Dude Ranch, which is in Moose. And I'm not kidding; it is really the name of the town."

We finished our beers, said goodbye to Hank, and told him we would try to stop on our way back. We went to the dusty corner he told us about and met the driver who told us to hop on. We had been saving up our money for months, and we were finally going to live like cowboys.

"I can't believe we're actually doing this," I said to Jimmy and Mario. "I've dreamt about being a cowboy since I listened to "Death Valley Days" on the radio. And I loved *Destry Rides Again* and *Billy the Kid* in the movies. Maybe we'll meet John Wayne or Tom Mix."

"Those guys are not real cowboys, you know," said Jimmy. "I don't think this dude ranch is going to look like the movies "

"I'm just glad we're finally getting away from our camp," said Mario. "I'm tired of digging ditches and chopping down trees all day."

The ranch was in the middle of nowhere, and it was nothing

like we had imagined. There were a few buildings and lots of tall grasses, wavering in the wind. Not far off were the jagged, snow-covered peaks of the Grand Tetons. As we got off the wagon, there were horses, cows, and chickens running around. The air was filled with the sound of birds chirping.

We were greeted by the owner, a man named Maxwell Struthers Burt. "You can call me Max or Burt, he said." He had a slight western drawl, but he seemed like he was trying to sound like a cowboy. He was tall and slim, dressed in tan slacks, shiny brown boots, a dark shirt, a yellow tie, and a white 10-gallon hat. "Where are you boys from? And what brought you here to Bar C?"

"We're in the CCCs in Yellowstone, and we're looking for adventure," said Jimmy. We told him where we were from and, just like Hank back in the bar, he immediately told us how much he appreciated what we were doing for our nation. He had a lot of questions, but when we asked him how much this stay would cost, he said, "Boys, your money is no good here. Consider this an all-expense free weekend."

We couldn't believe someone else was being so generous to us. I didn't feel like a hero, but maybe I was. We thanked him for his hospitality, and it wasn't until later we learned how expensive this place actually was. It was a resort for rich folks from the East who wanted to feel like cowboys and cowgirls, and for whom money was no object.

Max insisted it was his pleasure, and he wanted to help us in any way he could.

He walked us to our log cabin, which was on the edge of the forest, with a small stream running nearby. The cabin was small but cozy, with a fireplace in the living room and three small bedrooms and a bathroom. The walls were made of logs, and the floors were covered in hardwood. The windows were small, and the curtains were made of heavy fabric to keep out the cold. The furniture was simple but comfortable. He told us to get settled and said dinner would be ready in an hour. We unpacked whatever stuff we had and took a short nap. We were dead tired but happy, and we couldn't wait to start our weekend of cowboy fun.

The dining hall was filled with about thirty people, mostly wearing cowboy and cowgirl outfits. We sat down with some old folks, and I could tell by their fancy outfits they were probably rich. A few of them tried to talk like cowboys, just like Max did when we met him. Max's pronunciation was not bad; these folks were awful. I almost laughed to their faces, but opened my mouth. The three of us looked at each other and smiled. Once all the guests were seated, Max's wife gave us a speech.

"My name is Katharine Newlin Burt, and I am proud to know y'all. I wanna' welcome y'all to our humble Bar B-C Ranch. Max and I are hopin' you take full advantage of all of our activities while you're here, as we turn you dudes into genuine cowpokes."

She was also trying to sound like a cowgirl, but there was something about her pronunciation that sounded more Eastern and more educated. We were later to learn we were right.

"Your chow will be served in a minute, but we have three special guests, or should I say, dudes, with us tonight. Will Michael, James, and Mario please stand up?" She looked right at us and motioned for us to stand. We were taken aback, but slowly we rose out of our seats.

"These young men are members of the Civilian Conservation Corps, better known as the CCCs, and they have come here from a camp in Yellowstone. Please welcome these Brooklyn dudes with your applause for what they are doing to help preserve our beautiful nation. Thank you, gentlemen."

Everyone stood up and applauded as we slunk down in our seats, embarrassed by all the fuss. Katharine came to our table and shook our hands. The folks at our table had so many questions, and we all felt like celebrities for a night.

The meal started with a delicious onion soup with a thick layer of cheese on top. Next, the waiters brought each of us a Tomahawk Steak, each easily weighing two pounds. Then came a gigantic baked potato and a fresh salad. Even now, all these years later, I can still remember how juicy and tasty that steak was. We were fed well back in camp, but this meal, as well as all the meals that weekend, was amazing. As much as I was enjoying dinner, I did think of everyone, not only in Brooklyn but also those we passed in Hoovervilles who might be going to sleep hungry that night.

After dinner, we gathered around the roaring campfire and were entertained by a trio called the Carter Family. They sang a bunch of songs, including "River of Jordan," "Lonesome Valley," and "Worried Man Blues." The last one had a catchy tune and I remember the lyrics: "It takes a worried man to sing a worried song." It was a magical Friday evening.

The next morning, after a hearty breakfast, a guy named Jed and several ranch hands led a dozen of us amateurs on a cattle drive. First, we had to get up on our horses. Gary Cooper and Buck Jones made it look easy in the movies, but we all struggled to climb on, and we couldn't stop laughing and teasing each other. After lots of practice and several boosts from Jed and his cowboy helpers, we finally got the hang of it.

We rode our horses for hours, rounding up dozens of head of cattle and driving them to a new pasture. The cattle were restless and kept trying to break away from the herd. We had to be constantly on our guard, ready to stop them from running away. It was hard work, but it was a lot of fun. I had the feeling that the only reason we were moving them was for our enjoyment and that they would probably move them back for the next group of tourists/dudes. The sun was so hot as we rode through the dusty fields, but there was nothing quite like the feeling of riding a horse at full gallop, with the wind in your hair and the sun on your face. We finally reached the new pasture and the cattle were safely settled in. It was a great adventure, but it also gave me a really sore ass.

We went to the shooting range after lunch. I had never held a gun, no less fired one, so I thought this would be a lot of fun. Fitz, a lanky guy with white hair, was in charge of the range. He asked us a bunch of questions and showed us several six-shooters we could choose from. I picked a pearl handle Colt 45, Mario picked a Remington short barrel, and Jimmy got a Smith & Wesson long barrel. My gun felt so heavy in my hand and gave quite a kick when I fired it. We took turns firing at a bunch of bottles and tin cans about 20 feet away. I hit one, Jimmy hit three, and Mario struck out, but we kidded each other a lot and enjoyed the challenge. After shooting, I was glad to get back to our cabin, take a hot shower to wash out all the dirt I had collected, and then collapse on my bed.

We rested for about an hour when Jed knocked on our cabin door. Mario let him in and asked what he wanted.

"Mr. and Mrs. Burt would be honored if you would join them for dinner in their home."

"Sure thing," Mario said. "Is this something they regularly do for guests?"

"Actually, I've been here for about a year and a half, and this is the first time they've done it. Usually, they join the guests for dinner on the first night but after that, they dine alone. You boys must have made quite the impression."

The three of us were excited at the prospect of having a quiet dinner in someone's home, as opposed to the noisy mess hall at the camp and the loud crowd here. We changed into our dress uniforms and headed to their home, where we were greeted by Mrs. Burt. "Welcome, young men," said Katherine, as she opened the door. "I hope you are hungry because I've made a lot of food for you."

"Thank you for inviting us, ma'am," said Jimmy. "We have had a wild day, so I could eat a horse." Katherine laughed out loud. "I didn't mean real horse meat, ma'am."

"No, Jimmy. We generally save our horses for riding and such, but we do have some wonderful roast bison tonight. And please boys, just call me Katherine, or if you prefer, Kate, which is what my friends call me. Now come sit down in our den and have a drink with me and Max."

We walked into a huge room with high ceilings and big windows that let in a golden sunset. The walls were covered in amazing black-and-white photos of the Grand Tetons and Yellowstone. I went up close to one to check out the details, and Kate followed me.

"All of these pictures are beautiful," I said. "Where did you get them?"

"A young man named Ansel Adams stayed here last year, and offered to give them to us as payment for his stay. Ansel has a way of capturing the beauty of nature in a way that few others can. We were lucky to have him."

I looked at the pictures again, and I could see what she meant. They were all from the surrounding area, and they were absolutely stunning. I looked closely at one of the Grand Tetons. Although it was in black and white, he had captured the texture and breadth of those mountains with his camera.

"I'm so glad he gave them to you," I said. "They're really something special."

"We are glad as well. They're something to be cherished."

Then Max greeted us warmly and asked if we would like a Martini. We all agreed and he headed to the bar in the corner. I had only heard of Martinis in those sophisticated Hollywood movies, so this would be my first time having a grown-up drink in the home of two grown-ups. At that time, I had no experience with hard liquor, as we used to call it. All I had been drinking was beer, and due to prohibition, even that was hard to get.

Max handed each of us a V-shaped glass with a long stem with an olive in it, just like the ones from the movies. I took a sip and was a bit shocked by how strange it tasted. I could tell that my pals felt the same, but to be polite and try to act sophisticated, we all managed to finish them. There was a variety of cheese and crackers on a low table made out of real logs, so we joined right in, and that helped the drink go down.

We chatted about our backgrounds and theirs. Turns out, they were both from the East Coast: she was born in upstate New York, and he was born in Baltimore. He graduated from Princeton and even taught English there for a while, and her parents moved to Munich for a while, where she went to school. They met and married in Philadelphia, where they still had a house. But the best part was learning they were both novelists! Real, published novelists!

Over dinner, I asked lots of questions about their novels, and it seemed most of his took place in the business world in New York; hers were all set in the Wild West. Max was a bit of a stuffed shirt as he bragged about his thousand-acre ranch and how he had come to buy it with the proceeds of his books.

When one of us asked him why they came here, he said, "You must search for the loveliness of America: it is not obvious: it is scattered and when you find it, it touches you and binds you to it like a great secret oath taken in silence. I wish it were possible for me to see the Rockies once more for the first time." He paused and looked towards the windows and the sunset.

I wasn't sure exactly what he meant by all those words, but my feelings about the West were similar to his. I just couldn't articulate like he did.

"So, has the West changed much since you first got here?" I asked.

His reply sounded like he had said it before. "The old west is still there and can be found by anybody who really wants to make its acquaintance by automobile. But those automobiles engender a philosophy that is broad but never deep. They stand for halfway knowledge; you know the highways but you never know the land. You see the mountains but you never really get into them. You camp out but you never know the real heart of camping."

We all looked at each other, still not sure what he was talking about. Yet despite my short time out here, I wanted to get deeper into this land. I wasn't sure how to do it, but I wanted to try.

"Don't mind Max," Kate said. "He just likes to pontificate

when he is around impressionable people. Actually, he can be quite an asshole."

We three laughed at what Kate said; Max made some lame excuse about writing to his editor and left the room; I made a mental note to look up the word "pontificate."

"Mike here is a budding writer," Mario said, trying to change the subject. "He's been keeping a journal all about our CCC adventure."

Kate was interested and wanted to know more.

I told her my story beginning with how Miss Reed praised my essay and told me I had a case of wanderlust. I told her about my classes with Professor Booth and his comment to me about writing. I mentioned some of the escapades I had been including in the journal.

"I would love to be a writer someday, but given my family circumstances, I doubt I ever would have the luxury of time to even consider writing as a profession. My parents are poor and are counting on me for support."

I think I saw her wipe away a tear.

That seemed a signal we should leave, and we were all tired.

"Let's head back to the cabin," Jimmy said. "This has been a terrific evening."

As we started to leave, Kate touched my shoulder and asked me to stay a bit longer. "I have something for you." I thought it was a little weird and Jimmy gave me a funny look as he and Mario left.

We sat in the den and she said she needed to get something from her office and she'd be right back. I didn't know what to expect, but she soon returned with a copy of her latest book, *A Man's Own Country*. She wrote something in the book and handed it to me. I didn't read what she said until later. I stood up, thanked her, and got ready to leave.

"I only just met you," she said, "but I can predict you will become a writer someday. I could see the glimmer in your eyes as you were telling me about what you've been putting down in your journal and, more importantly, what you've left out. The stuff you left out will be that book. And if you ever need someone to guide you, I've included my phone number and address on a card in the book." She gave me a hug and a kiss on the cheek, saying, "You have a gift and you need to use it."

My head was spinning as I headed back. For one, I had never owned a book. Any book I ever read came from school or the library. The only book we had in our house was a dictionary. And the advice she gave me had me questioning my post-CCC life. Did it include following the Brooklyn Rules? Or was there something else here for me?

The guys were already asleep, so I got into my bunk and read what she wrote:

August 1933.

To Michael-- Take my advice: keep the literary light burning by putting your own life to paper. Fondly, Kate

The book's cover showed a man and woman, both on horseback—the woman was blindfolded and the man was leading her. It looked like he was going to surprise her,

I read the first chapter before I went to sleep.

On a Sunday morning of October in a Wyoming Mountain Valley, Micah MacKael left the bare little cabin, half office and half sleeping room, which as foreman of the Lazy B outfit, he ordinarily occupied and crossed a space of wildflowers and bunch grass recently grabbed free of sage, to the gate of the region known as "the Corrals."

Within this gate on a Sunday morning, the boys of the Lazy B sat on fence bars and doorsteps or lounged against the walls of smithy

and saddle shed, rolling their "makings," smoking and talking, soft and slow. Laughter was rarely audible, but it was in the air.

As Micah went by with his low, edged good mornin', laughter withdrew itself out of his world and conversation ceased. The cigarettes that were being rolled stayed in still brown fingers, the cigarettes that were being smoked sent up quiet blue spirals or went out. A stony change came upon these holiday loungers.

In the midst of the stillness, before the cold eyes and the unsmiling lips, Micah deliberately took down his bridle, let himself into the horse corral, and caught up with his own gray mare. He led her out, saddled her in a series of swift economical movements, pulled on a pair of ancient leather chaps over his life of his blue overalls and high-heeled shabby boots, buckled on his old spurs, screwed himself into a seat—the Westerners manner of mounting is the quiet half-turn of an upward screw—and jogged immediately away.

He rode at that tripping walk along the base of a steep sudden bank of sagebrush-covered earth about fifty feet high which, in a level drop from the wide plain above, stretched north and south as far as he could look, at a varying distance of two or three hundred yards from the edge of the Sliding River. The formation faced an identical one of the river's eastern side. Presently a little copse of aspens received Micah into his amiable twinkling protection. The watchful eyes and silent lips of the corral, the still spirals of blue smoke went out of range of that backward look he had controlled. Micah relaxed in his saddle and patted his mare's neck. "Grizzie! Good girl! He said gratefully.

I was in awe of Kate's writing. I wondered if I could even approach her beautiful style and use of details.

As I drifted off to sleep, I wondered if by giving me this book with the inscription, she was handing me a whole different life.

Rule 20
Do Not Leave Brooklyn

I got a package from Kitty and it was a surprise to me, and a letter from home saying another package was coming for me. I got that package a few days later. It had some tobacco from John, Butch, and Joe Rox. It made me feel good to think that my friends still thought of me. On Saturday I went to Marie's apartment as per usual and stayed overnight and had a great time and we plan to go to California to visit her relatives the following week. She was going to pick up her dad's car.

The next week we went to California. The country was beautiful. Every once in a while, we stopped and admired the scenery or to have a bite to eat. All at her expense. What a day that was. I was never more satisfied in all my life. We finally got to her aunt's house after driving ten hours. They was surprised to see us. At first they thought we were eloping and I nearly dropped from blushing. They owned a huge ranch house which looked like a palace. They did not have any children and they were very wealthy. All the time we were there, they treated us as if we were old friends. He even wanted to give me a horse for a present, but I told him I could not accept it because I couldn't take him back with me to Brooklyn. We stayed

*two days and they made us promise to come again before I left for
New York. I like those people a whole lot. We had a nice trip home
and was one day late at the camp. I went on as usual having sport
galore.*

*I also found out from her that she was very serious about me staying
in California for good and living with her folks. Right then and
there, I stated to her that I had no intention of staying there after
my term and that made her very unhappy. But she got over it before
we got back to Yellowstone, thank God.*

L et me try to unpack this journal entry because there's so
much going on. These were critical days for me, so I will try
to fill in some of what I left out thirty years ago. I'll begin with
Kitty and her package. She was one of my ex-girlfriends, and she
desperately wanted to get back together. It was obvious from her
letters, adorned with little drawings on the paper and the
envelopes and with all the XXXs and OOOs after her signature.
But I did appreciate the wonderful foods she sent, including
provolone and salami, a can of olives, as well as some biscotti, and
that Italian almond and nougat candy called torrone. I was happy
to share the food with the boys. The cigars were sent by John Cali,
Butch Guliano, and Joe Rocco, a part of a close group of friends,
that also included me and Jimmy. We five did so much together,
so getting that package reminded me of how much I missed
Brooklyn.

I was still averaging one long letter a week from Pauline about
what was happening in Brooklyn, but with all the girls I was
meeting in Montana and Wyoming, I was losing my interest in
her. Like the old expression, "out of sight, out of mind." Sure, I
was happy to open her letters, but between the hard work, the
fires, and the fun weekends, she was not on my mind. Next, there
was Marie and the trip to California. She and I had been in an

intimate relationship for a few weeks, and the trip was going to be monumental.

As we had planned, early on July 22, she came to pick me up. What I didn't know was that she would be driving a shiny red 1933 Buick convertible. The car was huge. I was stunned.

"Holy shit, Marie. I can't believe it."

"I wanted it to be a surprise, Mike. I picked it up from my father yesterday."

"I love it. What do they call that model?"

"It's a Phaeton. And wait until you drive it. "

Around 7 or 8, the boys gathered around to check out the car. They peered under the hood, and in the trunk and a few asked if they could sit in it. Marie was happy to answer their question and let them have some fun.

Jimmy took me aside, put his arm around me, and said, "Duke, we need to talk. You need to marry this girl right away. She's beautiful and rich, and she really loves you. Someone like her doesn't come around every day."

"I hear you, Jimmy. But I'm not sure I'm ready for that big step. I'm not even twenty, and it's an enormous world out there."

"Then move out of the way and let me go to California with her. I'll be married before we get back to camp."

I laughed and went back to the car. Marie tossed me the keys and said, "It's all yours today, Mike. Let's head out."

I got into the car, and as we drove off, I waved to the boys, literally leaving them in the dust. It was the fastest car I'd ever been in, and sitting with Marie made me feel so great. I never imagined any of this. I always loved cars and that '33 Buick was probably responsible for me being a Buicks man for my whole life.

Getting to California was tricky, considering that it was thirty years ago, before major highways existed. But Marie was a member of the newly-formed American Automobile Association (AAA) and she had gotten a TripTik routing map. We took turns driving and being the co-pilot.

As we drove with the top down and the wind in my hair, I saw the most breathtaking parts of America, from rugged mountains to vast deserts, and everything in between. I felt like I was living in a dream, and I knew that if it weren't for joining the Corps, I would never have had this experience. That would have been terrible.

We headed from Wyoming to Idaho, where we passed gorgeous mountains, and I made a mental note to visit there sometime before returning home in September. Idaho seemed desolate until we passed a herd of wild horses galloping across the landscape with a lone cowboy on horseback. As we continued south into Nevada, the desert gave way to rock formations and deep canyons.

We crossed into California. What a thrill it was to see the beautiful Sierra Nevada Mountains and the giant sequoias. Next, we passed near Yosemite National Park. After a quick stop for lunch and ten hours on the road, we arrived at a town called Chilcoot, where I met Aunt Sadie and Uncle Charlie.

Aunt Sadie had a strong Italian accent which reminded me of my mother's way of speaking. She and Uncle Charlie hugged us both, and as old Italians tend to do, kissed us both.

"Welcome to our home, Michael," said the aunt. "We love Marie, so if she loves you, then we love you, too."

She happened to mention that Marie loved me and had told them so. I was taken aback, but I just said, "Thanks for inviting us here. Marie has told me so much about you both, and I am looking forward to touring the ranch and farm here."

"It's getting dark, so let's eat. We'll have plenty of time in the morning for the grand tour," said her uncle. His accent wasn't so strong.

They knew we were coming, so they had a fabulous dinner ready for us. Uncle Charlie brought out a bottle of his best home-made wine. It was delicious. "I grew the grapes for the wine right here on my farm. California will be the next Barolo or Chianti region. I predict in twenty or thirty years we will outsell the wines from Italy and France."

I told him about the wine tasting we had at the World's Fair in Chicago. "This is so much better than any of those," I said. And I wasn't just trying to make him happy. Aunt Sadie had made a delicious lasagna and served it along with sausage, meatballs, and an excellent salad.

After dinner, Marie's uncle brought me to a bench outside where we smoked cigars and drank Limoncello. "I made this batch with my own lemons. Salute," he said as we clinked glasses. That was the first time I tasted Limoncello, but I knew it wouldn't be my last.

When it came time for bed, they showed us to our room. Our room! A room with one bed in a house that must have had plenty of bedrooms. These Californians were nothing like those prudish old-timers back home.

The following day's tour of their fifty acres was impressive: rows of lemon and orange trees, a vineyard of grape vines, several fig trees, and a thriving vegetable garden with every kind of vegetable one can imagine. They also had a small assortment of livestock, including chickens, pigs, and cows. "Someday this can all be yours," he said. "Sadie and I couldn't have any babies, so we think of Marie as our daughter. When we are gone, this will all be hers and, I hope, yours."

I didn't know what to say, so I said nothing.

We headed back on Monday morning with an overloaded basket of food, including bread, salami, and vegetables. "This was like being in heaven," I said as we pulled away from the house.

"Yes, it is, and you and I can have a wonderful life in Chilcoot, exactly like my aunt and uncle have." She reached over and kissed me. "We can have babies galore and pass the place onto them. Oh, dear Michael. I can't wait for your six months to be up." I mumbled something about how nice that would be, but my heart wasn't in it.

After several uncomfortable hours on the road, we entered Wyoming, and I knew what I had to do. I pulled the car over to the side of the road in the middle of nowhere, and turned it off.

Marie looked puzzled. It was bright and sunny, but what I was about to say was not easy. I turned to her, reached out, and held her hand. "I have something to say, Marie. I had a wonderful time with your folks and you, and California is a marvelous place. The offer that they made is generous, but I am sorry, this plan will not work."

I didn't say it then, but I was thinking of that first Brooklyn Rule.

"What do you mean? Why won't it work?"

"I am responsible for my family back home. My folks are out of work, my brother is sick, and since I am the oldest, there's a lot of pressure on me to step up and take care of everything."

"But they've gotten by without you while you are here. There's got to be a way to work this out. Let me think about it."

I put my arms around her. "Marie, you are one of the best things that ever happened to me. I've loved our time together, and I care for you so much. But I am not going to discuss this anymore. I will be going back to Brooklyn in September."

She pulled away from me and began to cry. I tried to comfort her, but that didn't help. So I started the car, and headed back to camp. She was quiet for the rest of the ride, but she gave me a hug and kiss when she dropped me off at the camp. "I want you to know I will be here if you change your mind. I love you very much, and I know we would have a great life together in California."

I felt like shit as I headed back to the barracks. I didn't know what to do next.

During the week, we did some work chopping trees, pulling out stumps, and making firewood. It kept us busy for 7 hours a day. At night we sat around, sang songs or played ball, went for walks with the boys to the Fishing Bridge or to the General Store.

One Friday night, my tent ran a dance. Our tent was called the
Savoy Plaza. As the mob of boys came in, the music by Paul
Metranga and Orchestra was the payoff. The captain and lieu-
tenants were the guests of honor. It was the talk of the camp.

A few weeks earlier, we heard about another camp that held
an actual dance with a full orchestra and lots of local girls.
We immediately decided we should host a dance, and we each
took on different roles, such as food, decorations, beverages, and
most importantly, working with Captain Collins.

I took charge of the music. I had heard about the Paul
Matranga Orchestra, a "territory band" playing in Billings. Territory bands were basically cover bands that popped up during the
Depression. Those bands traveled throughout remote areas of the
country to get jobs. The next weekend, I took the bus to hear
them play at an American Legion Hall. The hall was not much to
speak about, and the audience was mostly old folks who had come
to dance.

The music was terrific. These guys had lots of energy and
played a mix of country, jazz, and swing. They had the whole
audience dancing and singing along, and I knew they would make
our dance a success.

I went to meet the band leader, Paul Matranga. I told him
how much I enjoyed their performance, and I asked him if he
would be interested in playing at a dance that we were planning at
the CCC camp.

"I don't know," he said, "my band is very busy. And Yellowstone is way off the beaten track."

"Sure, but we work so hard all week and we need a good time
on a Friday night."

That story worked and he said he could fit us in. I had learned
mentioning the work of the CCCs had a positive effect on people.

"I do appreciate that. But how much do you charge?"

"It depends on a few factors. How long do you want us to play?"

"I'm thinking about four hours."

"That's a good length of time. We usually charge $75 per hour."

"That's a little more than I was hoping to spend."

"I understand. But we're a professional band, and we offer a high-quality performance. We're worth the money."

"I'm sure you are. But we're on a tight budget."

"Well, we could maybe work something out. What if we did four hours for $200?"

We agreed on a price and shook hands. I gave Paul all the details and my contact information.

The day of the dance finally arrived, and I was so nervous. I wanted everything to be perfect. The guys had decorated the tent with streamers made from tearing up some old magazines. Some of the boys had made sure that there was plenty of food and drinks.

The eight-piece band arrived in their bus right on time and set up their instruments. A few of the boys helped them carry the instruments, and we opened the curtain precisely at 8:00. Several busloads of girls arrived in really fancy dresses.

Paul and the girl singer named Paula did a great job of singing the songs, and they played nothing but the most popular ones. Everyone danced the night away. Paul began with "On the Sunny Side of the Street," and then went into "Puttin' on the Ritz" and "It Don't Mean a Thing (If It Ain't Got That Swing)." Before I knew it, the dance floor was mobbed and everyone was singing along. Then the band slowed it down with an appropriate song, "When It's Springtime in The Rockies" followed by "April in Paris," and "Night and Day."

They played all the greatest songs for more than three hours and ended with, "When Your Lover Has Gone" and "Goodnight Sweetheart."

So many guys, including the captain and the lieutenants, told us what a great job we had done. I felt so happy that my plans had worked out so well.

Rule 21
Finish Each Day With a Task Completed

One night we got another notice to go to another fire. I at once said to myself: another few days of hell. We were told to bring our blankets and working clothes and axes and shovels. We started out on trucks. After an hour of truck riding, we arrived at the lower base camp of the fire. We were fed and given food and started hiking up the mountain. It was starting to get dark and we were walking through woods and jumping over ditches and mud holes. Finally, it got dark and we couldn't see a thing. We only had one lantern and the guides on the horse had it. We couldn't keep up with him and we didn't have no light. We were struggling over everything. We couldn't even see the trees in front of us. Everybody was hollering for the guy to slow down. He did but we always lost him after a few minutes. Everybody was full of mud and water. I fell in a mud hole and had to get help to get out. It was real torture but I got a great kick out of it.

Watching everybody swearing and falling down every foot of the way. Some of the boys wanted to stop for the night and camp, but the guide said we had a few more miles to go so we kept going. We finally arrived at the fire base. It was another site to see the whole mountain all lit up by fire. It was after 1 o'clock so we were told to lay down and sleep until 5 o'clock to start fighting. That day plenty of food came up there thank God. And we ate plenty and we had good food for all the time we were there. We were there for five days and nights. We had the fire under control but we had to stay and see that it did not start again. We found out that there was nine different fires in the park at this time and all the camps were taking part in the fires.

———

After a tiring afternoon of planting seedlings, around 5:00 we were called to a new fire. We hadn't even had dinner, but we were told to quickly load our backpacks with our sleeping bags, mess kits, shovels, axes, and an extra pair of work clothes. I got on one of the several trucks, and we were off. The boys continuously cursed and complained on the way, foreseeing the magnitude of the upcoming fire. And it was enormous! As I wrote then, it took us about five hours to climb up a treacherous mountain in the dark before we could even rest.

One of my new friends, Tommy Genovese, was walking with me when we finally were able to stop. He and I were bitching and complaining all the way up. I was exhausted, but as we tried to fall asleep, we chatted a bit. I had known Tommy since we boarded the train back in New York. He was from Bushwick.

"We made it, Tommy," I said. "How are you holding up?"

"I'm fine, but I sure wish I was back in Brooklyn right now. I heard a few more guys refused to come on this trek, and they were probably going back home. I can't blame them. This night is the worst so far."

"Yeah, if I was home, I'd probably be coming back from a dance or a joyride with my boys. What about you?"

"It would still be warm there, so I might have spent the day at Rockaway Beach with my girlfriend, Sally. We'd probably go for a swim, build a sandcastle, and then have a picnic lunch. God, I miss her. What's the one thing you miss the most?"

"I could make a list: my mother's cooking and baking, my own bed, hanging out at the club, and even meeting the girls after church on Sundays. How about you, Tommy?"

"I'd be picking the plumpest figs from my father's backyard tree. They're so sweet and juicy, and they taste like summer. In about two months, I would help him cover up the tree for winter with blankets and tar paper. He and I have a specific ritual for doing it. We start by putting down a layer of blankets, then we cover that with tar paper. It might seem funny, but it's one of the favorite things to do with my dad."

I drifted off to sleep, listening to Tommy talk about his family and his home. It made me miss my family and friends back home. But I knew we were all ready to fight this fire together, and we would persevere.

Just as promised, the bugler woke us up at the crack of dawn. The sergeant told us we had 15 minutes to get ready. There were no latrines conveniently on this mountain, which meant we had to take a dump quickly in the woods. The trick we had learned was to find a fallen tree to sit on while doing our business. This was important because the ground was often wet and muddy, and we didn't want to get our pants dirty. We also didn't want to sit on the ground because it was covered in bugs. So, we would find a fallen tree and sit on it, facing away from the path so that no one could see us. It was not the most comfortable way to do our business, but it was the best option we had. And remember, we had to do this for five whole days.

Those next days were the most brutal and exhausting ones I've ever experienced. Every muscle in my body was sore. I couldn't imagine how hard the soldiers in the war had it, but it had to be just as grueling as fighting that fire. We were constantly exposed to smoke and heat, and the work was physically demanding. But we all pulled together and got the job done, and we had to be careful not to get burned or injured.

Finally, one day, authorities gave us the news that the fire had been contained and we were allowed to go back home. It started to snow as we were heading back to camp. It snowed all day long. It was a pleasure to get back and sleep in our bed again after sleeping under the stars with nothing over us but three blankets and sleeping on a bunch of pine boughs. It was some experience; the sky was beautiful. After I got back to camp, I got a bunch of mail from my friends and from home. My sister wrote and told me that my old sweetheart Nettie Parinello, has been over the house and looking for me. I was surprised. I answered all my mail including some from Jake Calderone who sent me some photographs of himself, Mary, and Sue and a large one of Mae West who he knows is my favorite actress and a letter that made me go hysterical with laughter. As usual he was a corker at writing letters.

O n the truck heading back, I started thinking about Alice, a girl I had met at last week's dance. The fire consumed my attention, making it hard to think about our relationship during those five days. The work had been physically and mentally demanding, but I felt proud when it was all over and I got home. We all referred to our camp as "home" by now, even though it was in the middle of Yellowstone. How could I have two homes?

When we finally got back to camp, I had a second letter from Grace about Larry and his tuberculosis. It was terrible news. I knew that we'd be getting back to Brooklyn soon, and I really hoped nothing happened to him while I was still here.

Dear Michael,

I'm writing today to update you on Larry's condition. As you know, they officially diagnosed him with tuberculosis in July, and he's been staying at home since then. Larry is doing well, all things consid-

ered. *He's following the doctor's orders and resting as much as possible. We try to keep the windows open all the time, and we try to help him out to the backyard now and then. He's also taking his medication regularly, and he's eating a healthy diet. Some TB patients are getting into fancy sanitariums, but we cannot afford that, so mama, Fanny, and I do our best to keep him comfortable.*

I know you're worried about him, but I want to assure you he's in expert hands. I'm here with him every day both before and after work, and mama and I are doing everything we can to help him get better.

Larry is a good patient. He doesn't complain about his medications and treatments, and he's always willing to do what we ask. But he's also scared and lonely. We have to keep him isolated in his room, so he misses his friends and activities, and he's worried about his future.

I'm trying my best to be there for him emotionally. We listen to his fears and concerns and offer him words of encouragement. We also make sure that he has access to books, magazines, and other forms of entertainment to help him pass the time.

I love him very much, and I'm determined to do everything I can to help him get better. I'll keep you updated on his condition. In the meantime, please don't worry. I'm taking good care of him.

By the way, Fanny and I went to visit Sammy at the reform school last week. He seemed different in a good way. I think and hope he has grown up some and has gotten past his wild ways.

We miss you and can't wait for you to come home.

Love,
Grace

The letter from Grace upset me. I knew little about tuberculosis or what they called TB, so I wandered over to the medical dispensary office to ask some questions. It was the place we all went to if we had cuts or rashes or any other issues, but I needed expert help. Doctor Ofri was on duty, and he was new there. He looked young, nothing like the regular doctors that were usually there. I introduced myself and asked a series of questions.

"Doc, my 18-year-old brother back home has been diagnosed with TB, and I have a question."

"Sure, Mike. What do you want to know?" He had a pleasant, encouraging voice, which made me feel comfortable.

"Well, what exactly is TB? How do you get it? And how do you cure it?"

"Those are three questions," he joked, trying to put me at ease. "Let me start with the signs and symptoms. TB patients can have fever, chills, night sweats, loss of appetite, weight loss, and fatigue. Is that what your brother is experiencing?"

His responses and his questions made me feel guilty. Here I was working and having fun in the perfect place, and Larry was stuck in bed, and I hadn't seen him in months. "Yes, that's what my sister told me. What happens next? What can we do for him?"

"It is an infection of the lungs, causing severe inflammation. The best treatment is bed rest and fresh air. There are some sanatoriums that treat it—one in Colorado Springs and one in Saranac Lake, New York. Scientists have yet to discover a medical cure; some antibiotics can offer partial help.

"Here's my biggest question, Doc. Can it kill you?"

"Not seeing your brother's full diagnosis, I cannot say. But unfortunately, it often leads to death. I'm sorry to tell you that, but it is the truth."

I shook his hand, thanked him, and went back to my bunk. I tossed and turned all night thinking about poor, helpless Larry. I believed I should be there. This thirty dollars a month wasn't worth it.

———

One night we went to a dance at Fishing Bridge Hotel. We were all dressed up in civilian clothes. We were having a nice time. All evening, the women were sociable. About 11 o'clock one of the boys asked a girl to dance and her escort passed a remark and asked him if he was a CCC man. The fellow said yes and the girl's escort said that no CCC man could dance with his girl. Whereupon, an argument started and the place was in an uproar. We all started to fight. The Rangers were summoned and we had to jump out of windows and porches in order to get away from getting locked up. After that night we all were barred from going to those dances. What a nasty break for us.

I got a new position as a chauffeur, which was another racket driving boys to and from work and also going to town for supplies and excursion trips which were 100 miles at least and over. And driving in those mountains was no cinch: narrow roads on top of mountains which means death if you make a mistake.

One day we took another trip to Gardner and raised hell. Most of the boys got drunk on beer and we're going wild stealing horses and making plenty of trouble. Finally, a few of them were locked up. The rest of them got on the trucks and we started back to camp. When we arrived we got a bawling out as usual but nothing was done about it, our captain being one of the best army officers in the US Army and a good sport. We all chipped in and got him a swell gift, and he was certainly glad to get it from us. Snow was coming down regular, but it used to melt in a day or so. Bear fights were very common especially black and brown against Grizzlies which ended in murders among them. And they hollered to make your blood chill.

August 30, 1933

I was in the hospital for a few days and I certainly enjoyed it. I had some trouble with my throat. There I met some pretty nurses and we used to sit out on the porch at night and tell stories. Finally, they got wise to me and sent me back to camp. I was sorry to leave and they were sorry to see me go, as so they said.

Rule 22

Jimmy died today. I have nothing else to write.

I couldn't find the words in 1933 to describe what happened to Jimmy or how it happened. That day and the days that followed were a blur. The memory of this horror still stays with me.

I was discharged from the hospital around noon. It was about 4:00, and I was resting in my bunk when Captain Collins walked in, looking very serious. From his demeanor, I knew something was wrong.

He was having trouble making eye contact with me. Finally, he said, "Mike, I'm afraid I have some bad news."

My initial thought was that something happened to Larry back home.

"Is it about my brother, sir?"

"No, son. I'm afraid it is someone close to you right here." Then he took a long pause. I wanted to yell out, "Just tell me already!" But I waited, as it was clear he was struggling to find the right words.

"It's Jimmy Cala. He was driving one of our trucks to pick up some boys out working when his truck veered off the road and tumbled down the cliff."

"Is he alright? What happened to him?"

"I'm afraid he didn't make it. He died at the scene."

"I don't understand. There was nothing they could do for him. Who saw it happen? How did they rescue him? Is he really dead?"

He kept giving details about how another driver had seen the crash and how they lifted Jimmy up to where an ambulance had arrived and more and more information. I sat there, frozen. I couldn't believe that this was happening. My best friend, dead? My best friend gone?

"I'm so sorry, Mike. There's really nothing else to say."

But I still had so many questions. "Did you talk to his family yet? Will they bury him here or send him home? Can I see his body?"

Collins mumbled some answers, but at that point, I wasn't listening. It didn't seem possible. Our friendship dated back to when we were 5 years old. He and I were inseparable growing up. We could tell each other stuff that we couldn't tell to anyone. We joined the Corp so we could be together. We were always together, working on the trail, laughing and joking like always. I wondered if I hadn't been faking it in the hospital, I would have gone with him.

And now he was gone. I didn't know what to do. I felt out of it. I wanted to leave this place and go to my real home and cry.

Later, Mario and the guys came over to console me. Mario and a few others were crying, and no one knew what to say to each other. We cried together, and we laughed together, and we shared memories of Jimmy, trying to make sense of his death. The word had gotten out, so the next day, several girls from town, including Sandy, Alice, and a few of Jimmy's girls, came to offer their condolences. Those that Jimmy had dated were especially upset.

Captain Collins called me in that day and explained how he had spoken to Jimmy's family, and he had arranged to transport his body back to Brooklyn.

"I know we still have a few weeks left," he said. "But if you would like to accompany his body on the train, I would allow you to go, and you'd still be paid for the entire month."

I didn't know what to say. Part of me wanted to get as far away from Yellowstone and the CCCs as possible. I pictured Jimmy alone on that train for what would be several days. But then I thought about Alice. Even though we had known each other for a short time, our relationship had taken us to a place we hadn't expected. We both were in love, and I couldn't imagine leaving her, especially now that I needed someone. Would it be right to abandon Jimmy for a girl? What kind of friend does that?

"Thank you for the offer, sir, but I'd rather stay here and finish the work we've been doing." The stuff about finishing the work was bullshit and we both knew it.

"But I would like to speak to his family, if I could."

He agreed, I had a long, weepy, and painful call to Brooklyn.

September 3, 1933

Dear Mr. and Mrs. Cala, Pauline, and Johnny,

Speaking on the phone the other day was hard for me because there was so much more I wanted to say about Jimmy and what he meant to me. As you know, we were best friends for over 15 years and we were as close as any two people could be. Spending six months together in Yellowstone brought us closer than ever. We ate together, worked together, laughed together, and went to town together, and I

*loved every minute. Jimmy was such a loyal pal, and we would do
anything for each other.*

*The captain asked me if I wanted to accompany Jimmy's body on
the train home, but I knew that being alone on that long trip with
only Jimmy on my mind would be awful. I decided to finish up the
month and keep busy with our work here. That didn't quite work
out well because no matter what I did, whether it was planting
sapling trees, clearing undergrowth to create trails and roads, even
going to the mess hall to eat, I could only think of him. When
someone told a joke, I said to myself, "I have to tell Jimmy that one."
Every morning and every evening, I would see his empty bunk next
to mine and imagine him still sitting there. I spoke with some girls
who knew him (and knowing Jimmy, there were a lot of girls) and
they told me how much he meant to them. And so many of the boys
in our camp came and shared such fond memories like "Remember
the time Jimmy did such-and-such" or "I'll never forget the day we
were in town and Jimmy did...," or "Remember what Jimmy said to
that nasty sergeant we had."*

You need to know how many people loved him here.

*I took a lot of photographs of him and the boys, and I will share
them with you when I get home. One of my favorites was when we
were sleeping away from camp, and a Black Bear cub came up to
our tent. The picture is Jimmy feeding the cub some biscotti that you
had sent him. A minute after I took that picture, the cub's mother
came looking for him. and we all closed up the tent and laughed
and laughed. Another was Jimmy with his arms around two pretty
Hawaiian girls who were touring the park. I can't wait to share
them with you.*

*Jimmy told me how much he loved you all and missed you so much.
We all loved the food packages you sent him that he shared with us.*

*He said he couldn't wait to get home and see you all and share how
we lived for those six months.*

*We should be heading home sometime this month, and I will tell
you more.*

Mike

P.S. I am really looking forward to seeing you, Pauline!

September 14

*We finally got news that we were going to leave on September 20th.
The boys went wild. Nobody could sleep for a few nights, breaking
beds and hanging them on trees was a hobby. And another fire
broke out again a few days before we were going to leave. We fought
like hell to get it out. We didn't want to get stuck out in the fire for
the 20th.*

*I got a truck one day and took a bunch of the boys out for a tour of
the park for the last time. Everything seemed as interesting as the
first time I seen them. I hated to leave the park. It was a beautiful
place and I enjoyed myself while I was there immensely. My only
thought was about how Jimmy would have felt.*

*That last night in camp, I went into town to say goodbye to Alice. It
was the hardest thing I ever did, and between losing Jimmy and
now losing Alice, I was ready to go home.*

September 20, 1933

*Left camp at 8 a.m. sharp on trucks to West Yellowstone. Arrived at
the station at 11 o'clock. After looking over the town for a few hours,
we were given seats, put on the train, and given our berths. And we
were ready to take off. We pulled out at 2:45 Mountain Time.
Went through the towns of Big Springs at 3:30, and later through*

Truckee. All very small towns also Island Park and Eccles and Pine View, another small town called Warm River. Then into Ashton Idaho a pretty nice town, at 4:50 o'clock. Chester, Twin Groves and St. Anthony. And then we stopped at a town called Pocatello. We stopped there for a few hours. A swell town. We had plenty of fun there with some girls and almost missed our train.

We then fixed our berths and went to bed. We woke up at 6:30 in a town called Rawlins, a nice-sized town. Stopped there for water and on our way again through deserts, and all we could see was sand and sagebrush. And then we went through lots of small towns such as Fort Steele, Wolcott, Hannah, Medicine Bow, Rock River, Lookout, Laramie, Hermosa, Sherman, Buford, Borie, Corlet Junction. We then came to a town called Cheyenne which was the capital and a large city. We walked around awhile etc. Archer, Hillsdale, Burns, Potter Connor, Sidney, Chappe, Julesburg, Colorda, a nice town, Big Springs, Ogallala, Buxton, Sutherland, Ofallons, Hershey. North Platte. We raised more hell and nearly missed the train.

Then we passed through Sugar City, Rexburg, Thornton, Lorenzo, Rigby, Ucon, Idaho Falls, Shelly, at which point I slept and stopped keeping track of where we were. I couldn't wait until we got back to New York.

Part Four
Brooklyn

Rule 23
Nobody Leaves Brooklyn

After a few days on the Union Pacific trip home, I stopped writing in my journal, so here are my recollections about what followed. We arrived at Grand Central Terminal at 7 AM on September 26th, just as the city was waking up. We gathered our gear and exited onto 42nd Street to board an army bus back to Brooklyn. As we rode through the city, I took in the sights and sounds of the morning rush hour. The streets were bustling with traffic and people going about their daily lives. We passed the Empire State Building on 34th Street. I craned my neck, and briefly saw the top. The air in the city was thick with exhaust fumes, along with the noise of cars and buses. New York was just as vibrant and exciting as I remembered. We headed south on Third Avenue for a while. The bus made a left turn, and there it was—The Brooklyn Bridge. The guys started yelling and cheering when we saw it. It was magnificent, and it meant "I was home."

Seeing the bridge almost blurred my memories of Yellowstone Park. The geysers, hot springs, bison, bears, mountains, forests, men, and girls were fading from my thoughts. I tried to recall the sounds of the geysers erupting, the wolves howling, the bison bellowing, or the elk bugling. But it couldn't erase all that. It never did.

I was home. But the reality was my adventure would always be a part of me. I had seen and done things that I never thought possible. I met new people and made new friends. I gained valuable insights about myself and the world. I had grown and become a better version of myself. I had seen death up close, but I had felt alive nearly every day.

Now it was time to come home and see my family and friends. I missed them dearly, and I couldn't wait to see their faces again. I knew they would be proud of me for what I had accomplished, and I couldn't wait to tell them all about my adventures.

Back at the base, after a lot of de-briefing, job counseling, and last instructions on returning to society, they formally discharged us. Earlier, I had called John Cala, and he was at the gate waiting for me. He smiled when he saw me. We gave each other a hug; I said I was so sorry that Jimmy had died; and we both tried to hold back tears. Then he grabbed my suitcase, and we headed out to his car. I was really excited to see him, and we spoke about so many things on our ride.

As soon as I walked in the door, I could smell the familiar aroma of mama's cooking wafting through the air. It was the smell of love, of comfort, of home. It was the smell of my childhood, of happy times spent with my family. It made me feel warm inside. Now I knew I was home.

The first person I saw was, Sammy, standing on the stoop. I learned that earlier that week, they had released him from the detention center for good behavior. He got excited when he saw me and gave me a strong hand shake. Then I saw Grace and Fanny, followed by hugs, kisses, and tears. Papa didn't get up, but he gave me a half smile, which was a lot for him.

Finally, I went to see Larry in his bedroom. He looked like he had been through hell. His skin was pale, his eyes were sunken, and he looked like he had lost a ton of weight.

"How are you doing, Larry?" I asked.

"Not so hot. I've been feeling really sick lately. My doctor said he's doing everything he can."

"I feel so bad for you. Now that I'm home, I will do whatever I can to help. Maybe later we can go outside and enjoy this pleasant weather."

"I'd like that," he said, though his voice sounded weak. "Just your being here is enough." I promised to check in on him regularly, and he seemed grateful.

I left Larry's room feeling sad and worried about him.

I walked into the kitchen, my stomach growling. The delicious Sunday sauce was on the stove, and my mouth watered. I walked past her, grabbed a chunk of bread, dipped it into the sauce., and swallowed it whole. The hot tomato sauce burned my tongue. I turned to Mama and embraced her.

"I missed you, Mama. And I especially missed your cooking." Mama smiled and hugged me back.

"I missed you too, *figlio mio*." Then, speaking in Italian, she told me how much she missed my appetite and how much she enjoyed cooking for me.

Later that night, I went over to Cala's family to pay my respects and to talk more about Jimmy. I had been dreading this moment, and it was about to become clear why. Pauline opened the door and hugged me so tight I almost stopped breathing. We both sobbed without saying a word. Our pent-up emotions about Jimmy's death came to light. We stood there for a long time, holding each other and crying, until Mr. and Mrs. Cala joined us in our tears. Sammy Stone, a close member of their family, was also there.

We all sat in the living room, on the plastic covered couches. Pauline and I sat together across from the others. She squeezed my hand hard. While we were wiping away our tears, John broke out a liqueur bottle of grappa and poured us each a small glassful.

"I want to make a toast," he said. "To Jimmy, the best brother a man could ever have had. We all miss you so much." We clinked our glasses together and said, "Salute." After we all took a sip, John continued. "And here's to Mike, Jimmy's best friend. Mike, we know you loved Jimmy as much as we all did. Welcome home."

I looked at Pauline as we took another sip, and she gave me an awkward smile. I could tell that she was feeling nervous. I wondered if she was thinking about the same thing that I was—where was our relationship going?

I started telling them some funny incidents that Jimmy experienced while we were away. There was still tension in the room, even though the mood lightened. I tried to find a balance between telling those funny stories and being respectful of everyone's feelings. I think it worked, because the others seemed to appreciate the effort. At least, they laughed a little. Then I got up and said I was tired and needed to get back to my bed that I had been missing for a long time. Pauline walked me to the door, and we stepped outside. Before I could say anything, she spoke.

"Thank you for coming tonight. I think you brought some cheer for my parents just by being here. I have something important to tell you. While you were away, I met someone and we've become serious. I still love you, Michael, but I love him too and he has proposed to me."

I was stunned. I had been looking forward to seeing her again, but I never expected this.

"I don't know what to say," I said.

"I know this is a lot to take in," she said. "But I wanted you to hear it from me first. I still love you, Michael, but I'm in love with him, too. And I think he's the one for me."

"Who is this person? Do I know him?"

"No, he's not from our neighborhood. His name is Chris Renino. He goes to Brooklyn College and is planning to be a teacher."

I nodded, still trying to process everything.

"I'm sorry," she said. "I know this is hard for you." She gave me a kiss on the cheek, and said goodnight.

As I walked down the stoop, I thought to myself, "She's going to marry a college guy, and I didn't even go to high school." I had doubts about marrying her, but I wanted to initiate the breakup.

Sammy Stone followed me outside. Sammy was a bit of a local

character. Nobody knew what he did for a living, but he seemed to have the newest cars and the nicest clothes. He was well-dressed and groomed, and he had a pencil-thin mustache and a charming smile. He was also friendly and outgoing, and he seemed to know everyone in town. He was a bit of a mystery, but he was also a popular figure in the community.

"Hey, Mike," he said in a hushed tone as if sharing something illicit. "Are you OK?"

"Well, Pauline just broke up with me, so I'm not so good now."

"Yeah, she told me she and Chris were getting serious. Sorry about that. How do you feel about a job with Coca-Cola? I know a guy who could make that happen."

I was taken aback and a bit skeptical. But Sammy was always true to his word. "Sure, but how would that work?"

"Well, let's just say he owes me a favor. Tomorrow morning, go to the plant on Flatbush Avenue, ask for Ralph Arpino, and tell him I sent you. If you have a chauffeur license, you could even be a driver."

I would like any job, but Coke sounded like a great one. While in Yellowstone, they granted me a license to drive trucks, so Coke might be okay with that.

I went to the plant early the next morning. Despite feeling nervous, I knew that I was prepared. When I arrived, I was greeted by a friendly receptionist, who asked me to sign in. She then took me to meet Arpino, the plant manager. He invited me into his office and offered me a seat.

"Well, Michael, I have heard great things about you from a certain individual," he said. "Am I correct in assuming that that individual is your godfather?"

I smiled, unsure of how to respond. Sammy Stone was a family friend, but not my godfather.

"I understand you were a truck driver in the CCCs. Is that correct?"

"Yes, sir. I drove fellow corpsmen around the camp and into local towns."

"That's all I needed to hear. Report to work here tomorrow at 8:00, and I will get you set up."

Could this arrangement be that easy? In 1933, jobs were so scarce, so imagine my shock when it happened. I reported the next morning, and they put me as a helper on a truck driven by a guy named John Bustelos. His route included most of Brooklyn Heights. We served restaurants, soda shops, and bars. At each stop, we had to pick up cases of empties and deliver an equal number of full cases. After doing this for a week, I understood the job.

Within a month, I had my own truck, my own route, and my own customers. I was working hard and making good money. I also learned a lot about the business. I learned how to deal with customers, how to manage my time, and how to stay organized. I also learned how to drive a truck in the streets of Brooklyn, as opposed to the dirt roads and mountain trails back in Montana.

I was overjoyed with my new job. I had already gotten over Pauline. I could finally support myself and my family. I could also save some money. I was feeling pretty optimistic about my future. I was confident that my life was changing.

All that remained was finding a woman, having kids, buying a house, and living happily ever after. Remember, those were part of the rules, I knew it wouldn't be easy, but I was determined to make it happen. I had always wanted a family of my own, and now that I was ready, I was going to make it happen.

Once Pauline and I were finished, I realized I had grown so much in the past six months that most of my silly local girls needed to be part of my past. I had some serious relationships at camp, so I needed to go to unfamiliar territory to look for love.

Several weeks later, I ran into Sammy Stone again, coming out of the barbershop.

"How are things at Coca-Cola?" he asked. "Have they made you plant manager yet?"

"Not yet, Sammy. It's only been a month, but I have my own truck and my own route, and I am making about $100 a month. I owe so much of it to you."

"That's great. Be sure to say hello to Ralphie Boy when you see him. And how is your love life? I hated to see you and Pauline break up, but those things happen. Any new prospects?"

"I'm so tired from work that I don't go out much anymore. So, no new girlfriends for me."

"I have an idea. I can introduce you to a girl I know who I think you'd like. Her name is Mamie, and she's a seamstress who works in the city as a dressmaker. She's a lovely girl, very kind and intelligent, and I think you two would have a lot in common. She's also very talented at her work, and I know you would appreciate her skills. I think you should meet her sometime."

"Since your instincts are good and your last introduction worked out so well, I guess I'm game. Where does she live?"

"She's right down the block at 558 Pine Street. She's the oldest daughter of Vincenzo Iannello, the local farmer. I'll arrange for you to have dinner on Sunday at her house."

I remembered that the kid that my brother Sammy was in trouble with was Angelo Iannello, though I didn't know the family. Mamie lived only a block away, but our paths never crossed.

I met a lot of great women, but I didn't find the right one until I met Mamie. She was everything I ever wanted in a partner: kind, funny, intelligent, and beautiful. She made me feel comfortable around her, and I knew I could spend the rest of my life with her. We got married a year later, and I've never been happier.

We've been married for twenty-five years now, and we have you three handsome sons. We moved to the suburbs and are living the American Dream. I wouldn't trade it for anything in the world.

I've had a successful career at Coke, because of my experience in the CCCs and a Dale Carnegie course my old boss Ralph sent me to. The course taught me how to communicate effectively with others, how to build relationships, and how to motivate and inspire people. These skills have been invaluable to me in my career, and they have helped me to achieve success in my current role as the branch manager at Coca-Cola's Westhampton, Long Island plant.

And so, my book and my story come to an end. I hope you three boys have enjoyed the journey as much as I did. Revisiting events that happened thirty years ago has been challenging for me, but I am glad that I did it. It has been a pleasure to share my world with you, and to let you get to know an important part of my early life.

Part Five
Yellowstone Redux

A Rule Not Broken

After writing that last chapter, I confess I left something out of this book. Something very important. I left out a secret that I've never shared before. I didn't know how to put it in writing. I had so many starts and stops, but none of them felt right. I wanted to tell you the whole truth. I wanted you to know a key part of that adventure I left out. So, I kept writing, and decided to write this letter to the three of you now that mom has passed.

That Friday night in early August I wrote about in Chapter 24 was the night I met Alice.

She was the prettiest gal I had ever seen, and that's no bullshit. I spotted her from across the tent, and when I looked at her, she was looking right at me. Her eyes seemed to sparkle in the light. Her skin was a warm, golden brown, and her lips were full and inviting. She had shiny straight black hair. She was wearing a simple yellow dress, but it looked stunning on her. She was the most beautiful woman I had ever seen.

I walked right up to her and asked her to dance, and saw her gorgeous green eyes. As soon as we got to the dance floor, we seemed to hit it off. The band was playing "Sophisticated Lady," which seemed so appropriate. These guys were not the Duke

Ellington Orchestra, but I didn't care. All I knew was that I was with the most beautiful girl in the place. Her body felt so warm next to mine, and her hair smelled fantastic. After our second dance, the band played, "It Don't mean a Thing if It Aint Got That Swing."

"Let's take a walk," I said. "It's too hot and noisy here. Let's find a quiet place to talk."

"Agreed," she said. "I sort of remember passing a little pond not far from here. Right?" She had the sweetest voice, and it was smooth and almost sensual.

"I know exactly where it is," I said, reaching out for her hand. "I will take you there." Her hand was warm and soft and gave me no resistance.

Only a few hundred feet from the tent was the pond, surrounded by several Weeping Willows that almost touched the still surface. We sat on a large rock and began what ended up to be a two-hour conversation.

"So, tell me your name," I began. "My name is Mike, but some of the guys call me Duke."

"I'm Alice. It's good to meet you, Mike. I'll call you Mike or Michael, if that's okay with you. You don't look like a Duke to me."

That made me laugh. "I don't even remember when or where I got that nickname, but I've had it since I was about twelve. My mother is the only one who calls me Michael, except she says it in Italian. She says, *'facci brutto, Michele,'* as she pinches my cheeks."

"What does that mean?" she asked.

"Actually, it means *ugly face*, but it's just her Italian way of having fun with me and saying she loves me. If she really wants to give me a left-handed compliment, she says, *'faccia de cane'* which means dog face. It's just an Italian thing."

"That's so funny. Tell me more about her and everything else about you."

"Both my parents were born in Sicily in Italy and came to America when they were about my age. My father used to work as a tailor in a huge department store, but because of the Depression, he lost his job, I have two younger brothers, Larry and Sammy, and two younger sisters, Fanny and Grace. I turned 20 last week. I was born and raised in Brooklyn, New York."

"Tell me more about your family and friends. I want to know what Brooklyn is like." She was so easy to talk with, and was so interested in whatever I said. She asked about my Italian neighborhood, our Italian food, and my Italian friends. No matter what I said, she just loved it all.

"Tell me about the CCCs," she said, "Why did you join them? What are you getting out of it?"

"The truth is I was desperate back home. I had my friends and family and a lousy job selling newspapers. I didn't make much money, certainly not enough to settle down and have a family of my own. There were no well-paying jobs available, and the Depression seemed like it would never end."

In the moonlight her eyes were looking at me in such a caring way. She understood my situation.

"When I heard about the CCCs and a chance to earn some decent money for my family back home, I was one of the first people to join."

"I am so glad that you did," she said. "Otherwise, I would never have met you." At that point, I leaned over to her and gave her a kiss. She kissed me back, Neither of us said anything for a short while.

Finally, she broke the ice. "Tell me what your typical day here is like. I want to know everything."

Her easy and comforting way of speaking was unlike that of all the Italian girls back home. Rosie and Bessie and Sarah and Amelia and all the others were fine, but Alice was worlds away. And even Marie here in Montana, with whom I had such an intense physical relationship, didn't come close.

I was smitten.

She asked questions and made me feel she was interested in everything. I can't describe her accent, though I later learned how it came to be. I told her all about the camp and how we spent our typical day. But she wanted to know more.

"Tell me about New York City. Have you ever been to the Empire State Building? Have you ever been to Radio City and the Statue of Liberty? What is Broadway like?" She had recently seen a newsreel about New York and was so excited to meet a New Yorker. I filled her in on the City, and all she kept saying was that she wished she could see it someday. I needed a break telling my story. "Okay, enough about me. Tell me all about you."

She seemed hesitant at first. "I work at the Yellowstone Victorian Inn in Gardiner. Me and the other girls live in the hotel's dorms which is really convenient. I am sort of a receptionist and maid, and sometimes, I wait tables in the restaurant there."

I asked her for more information about her family, she began to tear up, so I stopped asking. It sounded like the band was finishing up, so we went back to the dance and made a date to meet the next Saturday at the hotel in Gardiner.

I started seeing her every chance I could get, and I couldn't stop thinking about her. We spent a few nights together every time her roommate was out of town. We were in love and we wanted to tell the whole world. I couldn't imagine our lives without each other. I wanted to wake up next to her every morning and go to sleep next to her each night. We wanted lots of children who would grow up in this beautiful land. I wanted us to share everything with each other, from the big moments to the small ones. I wanted to grow old together and watch our love grow over time.

Then on Tuesday, August 10, I received a long letter from her. While looking through my CCC stuff last month, I found the actual letter in her perfect handwriting, so I'll just include it here.

Dear Michael,

I have not been totally honest with you regarding my family and my heritage, and there's a reason. This will be a long and painful letter to write because I am going to tell you the whole story. I know if I tried to tell you in person, I would cry the whole time. It is a sad story.

The truth is, I am a Cheyenne Indian. There, I've said it. It's a sentence I've been wanting to say to you since we met at the dance. If you want to stop reading any further after hearing this, I will understand, and you won't ever hear from me again.

I was raised on a reservation in Montana with my mother. I never met my father, but my mom always said he was a handsome white fur trader. I wish I could have met him, but I guess I'll never know. When he met my mom, he was in between hunts, so he could stay with her for a while. She told me the two of them were madly in love. She even showed me a picture she had of the two of them together. But soon after I was born, he headed out, apparently seeking more furs somewhere. He swore to my mother he would be back within a year, but he never did. She was sure something had happened to him.

Over the next 9 years, my mother and the circle of women in our tribe taught me so much about who we were. They considered my tribe Northern Cheyenne. Our reservation was in the southeastern part of Montana. Our ancestors originally lived in Minnesota territory, but about 50 years ago, soldiers came and moved us. My people were known as expert hunters and therefore, we always had a supply of meat. My mother and the other women would go searching for roots and berries and other edible plants, and when I was about 4, I came along to learn how to search out these foods. I also learned about tanning hides and making and decorating clothing from the women in our circle.

I had a small group of friends there and we would play games and sing together. But my favorite aspect of our culture that my mother taught me was the love of our beautiful language. She gave me my name, Aponi, which is Cheyenne for "butterfly." I loved the way the language sounded, and I loved how it could be used to express so many different things. I also loved learning about the history and traditions of my people through the language. My mother was a great teacher, and she instilled in me a love of my culture that I will always cherish.

Yes, Aponi is my real name, Michael. I loved my name. I was not known as Alice until much later. My mother taught me the Cheyenne language, which was called "Tséhésenéstsestótse," and it is a beauti-ful, descriptive language. I loved learning some beautiful-sounding words like mahpe for "water," enemene for "singing," hahóo for "thank you," haaahe for "hello," and nemehotatse for "I love you." Those are about a few I remember, and you'll understand why I've forgotten more of them later in this letter.

When I was 9 years old, a man and woman from the government came and took me away. It was the last time I saw my mother. I sometimes have nightmares about that day and those people who took me. They were both wearing tan uniforms like they were in the army or something. The woman was probably in her early 20s with ginger-colored hair, and I remember she had red nail polish. She was thin and had a phony smile the whole time I saw her. The guy, who seemed in charge, was probably in his 50s and had several bright tattoos on his arms, mostly of things like anchors and mermaids. He wore a dirty gray cowboy hat. My mom held me tight and told those two they couldn't have me.

"We will be taking her to a nice school where she will learn skills that will help her get a good job," the woman said. "And when she returns, she can help support you and the rest of the villagers."

"You really have no choice," the tattooed man said. "The govern-

ment will stop giving you and the other villagers any rations or help if you refuse."

This had to be a very difficult decision for her to make, but, with tears in her eyes, she gave up. She must have been heartbroken to do this, but she thought it was the best thing for me and our family.

"Don't worry," the nail-polished woman said. "We will bring her back a few times a year to see you. So just think of this as an out-of-town school."

That was a lie. I never saw her again.

They were despicable people. They took me and several other girls around my age on a long bus trip to a Catholic Indian boarding school in North Dakota. We all cried most of the way, not knowing what awaited us. Remember, I was only 9 at the time.

The nuns running the school were cold and harsh. The first thing they did was to cut our hair and burn our native clothes. We were forced to speak English and forbidden to speak Cheyenne. We were also forbidden to practice our Cheyenne culture.

I was miserable at the boarding school. I missed my mother terribly. I cried myself to sleep every night. But I knew that I had to stay strong for her. I had to survive. I spent eight years at that school. During that time, I never saw my mother again. I didn't even know if she was alive. When I was sixteen, I finally graduated and was told to go to Yellowstone where a job at the hotel was waiting for me. But first, I was determined to go home and find my mother. I hitchhiked all the way back to our reservation. When I arrived there, I was heartbroken to learn that my mother had died a few years earlier. I was all alone.

That is my story.

Even though I was separated from my mother at a young age, I am grateful for the life I have. I am still a proud Cheyenne woman. I am a survivor. I would like to see you again, but I will understand if you feel that you cannot.

Affectionately,

Alice

I knew something about Alice was different, but it certainly shocked me when I read her letter. It came on a Wednesday, and I pondered my next move for days. Should I go to Gardiner and meet her on Saturday or just stay in camp to avoid seeing her? There have been significant changes in the past thirty years. As a country, we have lost some of our racist tendencies, but back them, most people treated Indians with disdain.

I knew some guys would make fun of me for seeing an Indian, as I had heard comments like "redskins" or "Injun" and "papoose" or the really nasty slur, "prairie nigger" when some guys referred to native people. Even though I wasn't thinking that far ahead, I imagined what would happen if I ever brought her back home to Brooklyn, where racist slurs about anyone and everyone are used in everyday speech, whether someone was talking about Blacks or Irish or Puerto Ricans or Jews. Or especially we Italians. What would my family and friends think of her? How could I subject her to so much hatred? I thought about the Brooklyn Rule: Marry an Italian girl (preferably a Sicilian) and live near my parents.

Finally, on Friday afternoon, I had a talk with my two closest friends, Jimmy and Mario. We sat far away from anyone else, and I gave them Alice's letter. They read for a long time.

Jimmy simply said, "Holy shit!"

"That's how I thought you'd react," I said. "Now tell me what you really think."

Mario spoke first. "I feel so sorry for her, and I guess I feel bad for you. It might not be that bad if you keep seeing her. I mean, she's real pretty and doesn't look like an Indian. And she speaks real good, too. So, what if you just keep it between us and say nothing?"

"But wait a minute," Jimmy said. "Mario, you've got to be kidding. Duke, you know precisely what's expected of you. End the relationship and forget about her completely. Imagine if you got too serious, and you brought her home to meet the family? This has to end. Now!"

Jimmy walked away, at which point Mario looked at me with concern.

"What would happen if you didn't go home at all?" he said. "Sandy and I have been talking about me staying out here with her. I mean, if you love her, don't go back to Brooklyn."

I sighed. "I know. But I have to. My family is there. My friends are there. My whole life is there."

"But you could start a new life here with Alice. You could be happy here."

"I don't know. It's not that easy. I have to think about my family and my sick brother. They are all counting on me to get a job and help support them."

"But what about your happiness? What about what **you** want?"

"I don't know. I need some time to think."

Mario patted me on my back. "I know you'll make the right decision."

The conversation made me think a lot, but didn't provide any helpful guidance.

I said nothing at all except to thank him for his advice. I took the letter back and headed to my bunk and read it again. What a dilemma. What should I do?

That Friday night, I surprised Alice by showing up at the hotel. She came out back for a while and gave me an enormous hug.

"I wasn't sure you'd come," she said. "I thought my letter scared you away."

"Your letter was so beautiful, and I love how honest you were." I touched her cheek and followed it with a gentle kiss.

"I love you, Michael," she said. "I've never met anyone like you."

"I love you too, and your letter changes nothing, except maybe I love you even more now." She completely broke down and cried. I held her tight and tried to calm her down.

Two weeks later, we went on a double date with Sandy and Mario to the Grotto Restaurant in Gardiner. Before we could order our meals, Sandy blurted out, "Me and Mario are getting married!"

I knew they were close, but I didn't expect that. Neither I nor Alice said anything.

"We want you both to be at our wedding party," she said. "Alice, would you be my maid of honor?"

Mario added, "Mike, I want you to be my best man."

Alice and I stared at each other with open mouths, but of course we agreed. Over dinner, they told us more about their elaborate plans. They had already planned to marry at Mammoth Chapel, a week before our CCC time ended. They planned their honeymoon at the Chico Hot Springs resort. Their plan was to live in a cabin close to Gardiner, with Sandy working at the hotel and Mario applying for a park ranger position.

"We hope that you folks can join us here," Sandy said. "We'd love to have good friends nearby."

We didn't respond, but later that night, Alice and I discussed Sandy's offer. Maybe they were right. Perhaps Alice and I do belong here. With Jimmy being dead, maybe I could break the rule, say goodbye to Brooklyn and my family.

We continued to see each other as often as we could. On weekends, we would go on picnics or hikes together. We saw parts of Yellowstone that I had never seen before.

Back at camp, we were all getting ready to pack up and head home. We had heard we would get on a train on September 19th. It was time to decide. The one thing I knew was that bringing her home was not an option. Do I stay here with the woman I love, or do I do the expected thing and head home? I knew that if I stayed, I would give up everything I had ever known. My family, my friends, my whole life. But I also knew that if I left, I would probably never see her again. She meant everything to me, and life without her was unimaginable. But I also knew that I couldn't just abandon everything I had worked for. I felt torn in two, and didn't know which way to turn. I didn't know how to make things right. I felt like I was in a lose-lose situation. But leaving her without an explanation was something I couldn't and wouldn't do.

On Sunday, I actually attended Mass and did something I almost never did. I prayed for an answer.

I made my decision.

The night before we were to leave for home, I got a ride to Gardiner and met Alice. We walked to a quiet place behind the hotel and sat on a log. When I told her I was going home, she wept, and I joined her. It was awful.

"I want to come with you, Michael," she said as she continued to cry. "If I can't go on the train with you, I will save up some money and come as soon as I can."

"I'm sorry, but I won't let you do that. You don't know what people are like there. As soon as people discover you are Cheyenne, they will ridicule you unmercifully. My family often makes hurtful racist remarks, and I used to do the same."

"So why don't you stay here just like Sandy and Mario are doing? Maybe the two of you could get jobs together."

That painful conversation went on for a long time, but finally, we kissed and I left. I walked away from her, and didn't look back. I felt sick to my stomach the entire time. I couldn't believe what I had just done. I just wanted to get away as soon as possible.

That final conversation was on September 19, 1933, and it continues to haunt me to this day.

There's a scene in one of my favorite movies, *Citizen Kane* about such a memory. A man named Bernstein says:

"A fellow will remember a lot of things you wouldn't think he'd remember. You take me. One day, back in 1896, I was crossing over to Jersey on the ferry, and as we pulled out, there was another ferry pulling in, and on it there was a girl waiting to get off. A white dress she had on. She was carrying a white parasol. I only saw her for one second. She didn't see me at all, but I'll bet a month hasn't gone by since that I haven't thought of that girl."

I end my saga with this anecdote because I think about Alice every day. She wrote me a letter soon after I returned home, but I didn't even open it. I tried to forget about her, but I couldn't. She was always on my mind. I still think about her smile, her laugh, and the way she made me feel. I know I should have written to her, but I was too afraid. I was afraid of what she would say, and I was afraid of what I would say.

Over the past 30 years, I have had several false sightings of her in crowds, only to realize when I got closer to some slim young woman with jet black hair, that it was not her. I am confident that I will never see her again, but I will never forget her. I frequently ponder if she is still in Montana, or if she has met someone who loves her as much as I did, or if she ever got to see New York. Or if is she still alive? I hope that she is happy and healthy, wherever she is.

Every weekday, I wake up, have breakfast, and go to work. But my thoughts keep going into the past. I think about all the things I've done, all the people I've loved, and all the mistakes I've made. I wonder if I could have done things differently. I wonder if I could have been a better person. But I know that I can't change the past, so I just keep on keeping on. I try to focus on the present and the future. I try to be the best person I can be. And I hope that one day, I can finally let go of the past and move on.

While coming home on the Union Pacific, I finally finished *A Man's Own Country*, the autographed book that Katharine Burt had given me on that wonderful night at the dude ranch. She never knew the impact her words had on me, and how they inspired me to write this book.

Her book is a charming story about Micah, who I mentioned in the first pages, and Eugenia Aurelia Mooreen, a schoolmarm from Scotland. Eugenia who comes from a fancy family back home, uses a fake diploma to get a teaching position under the alias, Patty Pitcher. She and Micah fall in love despite their strong differences. Here's how the book ends with Eugenia talking about their unlikely future lives together:

"You and I Micah will keep on being ourselves—a Westerner and a schoolmarm. We will be Micah and Alias Patty to the end of our lives. Perhaps our children will want to go East and study and be different...They can. But you and I are runaways and outlaws, and that's what we will always be. You and I together, Micah."

He sighed deeply, moved his big hands in the sagebrush, and then looked up at her and dropped his head upon her knees. "Tis your country lady," he said, "and I'm your man."

Was it possible that Kate's words were an omen, trying to tell me something?

The End

Author's Note

This book is a recollection of events that happened in 1933. It is about my father, Michael Charles LoMonico, a young man who joined the Civilian Conservation Corps, trained in Brooklyn, and traveled to Yellowstone National Park, where he spent five months. There he learned how to live life to the fullest and how to become a man. But there he also witnessed death and loss. He died in 1965, leaving his CCC journal a CCC banner, some letters, and a set of varnished elk antlers.

The book includes excerpts from that journal, and I added what he might have left out and what it might have meant to him. Those reflections and commentary are all mine and are completely fictitious.

But this book represents those three million young men, from New York to California and all states in between, who joined the CCCs between 1933 and 1942 and were deployed to all 48 states, thus helping to shape America.

This book has been marinating since I discovered that journal in 2003, and I have written several variations before arriving at the present version. I think I finally got it right. There have been many friends who have read parts of this and given me excellent suggestions and helped me find my final direction. Among them are Maura Charles, Kate Breen, Glenn Wallace, Chris Renino, Bob Monteleone, Ada Graham, Joe Perlman, Annette Thies, and June Keenan.

I also must thank Ghia Szwed-Truesdale, who was the first to read and edit an early draft and suggested that focusing on the Brooklyn Rules was the key. She said my story needed to be told and that it will make a great movie. She gave me the final push I needed to complete this book.

I especially want to thank my exacting editor, Savannah Hinson Rivas, who magically transformed this book to a far better one. And my former student and author, Amy Wasp, a true professional, who converted my messy Word doc to an excellent interior design. I also want to thank so many friends who helped select and edit the cover design.

My biggest supporter is my wonderful wife, Fran LoMonico, who read several drafts and never stopped believing that I had something important to write. She made it all possible. This book belongs to her as well.

Michael LoMonico, 2024

About the Author

* * *

Michael LoMonico, the author of the YA novel, *That Shakespeare Kid*, and two reference books, *Shakespeare 101* and *The Shakespeare Book of Lists*, has turned to his Italian heritage with *Brooklyn to Yellowstone*.

He has demonstrated a passion for all literature, especially Shakespeare, by writing and speaking about the Bard, leading teacher workshops in 40 states as well as in Canada, England, and the Bahamas. For almost 20 years, he taught a course, "Shakespeare Teaches Teachers" at the Brooklyn Academy of Music (BAM). He was a Senior Consultant for the Folger Shakespeare Library in Washington, DC. He was the founder and editor of *Shakespeare* magazine, published by Cambridge University Press and Georgetown University. He was an assistant to the editor for all three volumes of the Folger's *Shakespeare Set Free* series, published by Washington Square Press.

He was a guest on the cable TV show, "Italian America Long Island" discussing Shakespeare and Italy, connecting his knowledge and passion for Shakespeare with Shakespeare's fascination for all-things Italian. He was invited back to discuss and demonstrate how to make Caponata, the traditional Sicilian dish, using his mother's recipe.

Michael taught English in high school and at Stony Brook University. He lives on Long Island with his wife Fran.

Made in the USA
Middletown, DE
06 September 2024

60452126R00124